CONCEALED - LEXI

A VAMPIRE BLOOD COURTESAN BOOK

ROSALIE REDD

CONCEALED - LEXI
A Vampire Blood Courtesan Book

By

Rosalie Redd

For permissions contact: Rosalie@rosalieredd.com
Cover Design: Raven Blackburn
ISBN: 9781944419226
United States of America

CHAPTER 1

LEXI

 eath.

How appropriate.

The tarot card reader, Danae, laid out the five cards I'd selected from the deck, and the last one, a picture of what appeared to be a girl sleeping, seemed innocuous enough except for the skeleton at the top and the word 'death' at the bottom. I raised my gaze to Danae's eyes. Small pools of brown, they appeared knowing, as if she could see the evil, cancerous tumor on my spine. Yep, death was a fitting card for me to draw tonight.

Danae glanced at the dark picture window that graced the old Victorian house. The porch light cast a subdued yellow glow over the lawn and onto the tall pines lining the edge of the property. She shifted in her seat, and the old wood creaked. With a smile, she reached across the table and wrapped her fingers around my shaking hand. "Lexi, don't take the cards literally. There's much under the surface."

The rich sandalwood incense burning on the table eased into my lungs, but did little to calm my nerves. Damn you, Miranda, for bringing me to Brinnon.

"A few days away to hike and spend some time in nature will do you good."

Yeah, right. Instead of spending our time in the beautiful forests that covered Washington's Olympic Peninsula, we were here for a tarot card reading. My best friend had set me up. Miranda never did anything halfway, and her belief in the power of tarot cards followed suit. As if some magical mojo could cure me.

Seated next to me at the round table, I cast a dagger-eyed glance at her. She shrugged, and sadness fluttered across her expression. With dark hair, brown eyes, and olive skin, she was a bombshell beauty. My blonde hair, blue eyes, and pale skin were in sharp contrast, but I'd had enough guys ogle me. I was no slouch either. It would be nice though if one would take the time to get to know what was inside before hitting on me.

Not that it mattered anymore. My cancer would age me in ways I couldn't even imagine, especially if I didn't get the recommended radiation treatment. Months they'd said. My chances of survival, a long shot. Maybe I was a fool to have any hope I'd beat the tumor, but hope I did. "So what do the cards mean?"

The light from the elegant antique lamp cast a warm glow over the table, accentuating the cards' gilded edges. Danae placed her finger along the first of the five spread out like a fan over the deep mahogany. The card displayed a picture of a blindfolded woman surrounded by eight swords, several blades embedded in the rocks. "You asked what your future held. This card represents your current situation or dilemma. What do you see in this card?"

"I'm blindfolded. Does that mean I can't see? What about the swords? Why are they in the—" I cringed at the blood red robe that cloaked the woman and the three ominous swords piercing the snow. Just like needles.

A smile tugged at Danae's mouth, and her dark eyes flashed with a bit of humor, but it faded. "The Eight of Swords is an air sign. The meaning varies, but most often it is a symbol of bondage, dissolution, or loss of hope. Perhaps you're experiencing a time of difficulty, or trouble may lay ahead with illness or misfortune. Does any of this ring true for you?"

Dry and thick, my tongue was stuck to the roof of my mouth. Clearing my throat, I nodded. "I'm having health...problems and don't know how to proceed."

Danae placed her hand over mine once again. "That's tough. Let's see if we can find solutions and a path forward for you. Be careful, indecision could make matters worse, but this is the time for you to rally your strength to overcome the adversities you face."

Miranda leaned forward. "How so?"

Danae raised an eyebrow. "Listen to the cards, there can be much truth and wisdom within them."

Before Miranda could say anything more, I nudged her foot, our sign to 'let it go.' Best friends since sixth grade, we'd been through everything together. I didn't know what I would've done without her, especially since my father passed away.

I'd just graduated from the University of Utah's school of dance a few months ago when I'd received the devastating news of the car crash. My mother had died during my birth, so it had been just me and Dad. Had I known he was in debt up to his eyeballs, I never would've left Oregon and selected such a prestigious school. Returning home to Portland, the only job I could find was as a waitress at Hooties. Not long after, I discovered the first inkling of my illness, a worsening ache between my shoulders.

Danae tapped her fingernail against the table, drawing my attention to the next card, the one that looked like a couple staring through a church window, five coins lodged in the arch. She trailed her fingers over the golden coins. "The second card tells of your present wishes. For you, the Five of Coins illuminates your desires. Like the supplicants in this church, you may yearn for money or a fix for your dilemma, but beware, what you think you want may not be what you need."

Danae's brown eyes bore into me, as if she understood me far better than I knew myself. I couldn't look away.

"On your journey, misguided goals, poor decisions, or lack of decisions could lead to destitution and misery. Ill health and misfortune may await you. Do you see the lush evergreen forest behind the red-clad woman? There may be help nearby despite your rocky path."

I furrowed my brow and studied our tarot card reader.

Her gaze didn't waver. "Did you have a question or are you ready to continue?"

I glanced at Miranda. She raised an eyebrow, letting me make the decision. My attention drew past the fourth card to the final one, the death card. A shiver started at the base of my spine, tripped up my back, and raced over my shoulders. All I could think about was my future, or lack thereof. I swallowed and nodded. "Please, go on."

Danae traced her finger past winged angels swooping in circles and around a wooden wheel, stopping to rest at the woman cradling a small baby in her arms. A soft sigh escaped the tarot card reader's lips. "Ah, the Wheel of Fortune. Everything goes in a circle. What you lose on the swing, you gain on the roundabout. You cannot have good without bad or light without darkness, but do not dwell on misfortune, look instead to future joys. Perhaps an interesting opportunity will arise for a fresh start or the beginning of a new path or venture."

"A new path?" I choked on my words.

Danae tilted her head, a knowing gleam in her eye. "What is your dream?"

"To dance." The words tumbled from my mouth. "My father loved ballet. He was my staunchest supporter, encouraging me every step of the way..." I couldn't complete my sentence. His death was still too raw. Tears stung my eyes.

Danae tapped her finger against the next card. The tip of her red fingernail landed on the image of the mother and child. "Is dancing what's most important to you?"

More than anything I wanted someone to love me for who I was on the inside. If kids came later, well, that was a bonus. A twinge tightened my chest. Even if I weren't dying, I'd learned that men couldn't be trusted. Outside of my father who loved me without question, I'd had a string of boyfriends that tainted my view of the male of our species. Each one seemed more eager to explore my body than learn about my dreams and desires.

I cleared my throat. "Yep, dancing is my number one priority."

Danae blinked, but didn't press me. Instead, she focused on the fourth card, a picture of a moon in a forest setting with a deer, a rabbit, and a greyhound. "This is the immediate future. The moon, which wanes on the card, will grow full again in due course. Embrace that which darkness can bring then daylight will return all the sooner." She met my gaze. "Beware of hidden threats and enemies. If you have a secret, it may be exposed."

My throat tightened. This didn't sound good. "I don't have any enemies."

She studied my features. The dark circles under my eyes must be visible beneath my makeup. All of a sudden, my sweater seemed a bit too warm. I tugged up my sleeves, but couldn't hold her gaze. "I guess you could call my sickness an enemy."

"It's one you'll beat, Lexi." Miranda flipped her jet-black ponytail over her shoulder, and the tip smacked against the back of the wooden chair. "The money will come up, I know it will. Then you can afford the insurance."

Self-employed with debt, my dad missed a few payments, and the health insurance lapsed. No longer enrolled at the university,

I couldn't obtain coverage through them, and outside of the enrollment window, I couldn't purchase individual coverage, not that I could afford it anyway. Medicaid, well that was under-funded, and I'd be dead before I got through all the paperwork. "I've already been down that road. Insurance won't do me any good. What I need is a lot of money, quickly. Say," I gave Danae a lopsided grin, "you don't have a winning lottery ticket hidden under that last card for me, do you?"

Danae stifled a laugh that turned into a cough. The bout went on for several long seconds before she patted her chest and cleared her throat. "No, there's no lottery ticket, but I might have something else for you, after the reading."

My heart picked up speed to match my curiosity. Suddenly, I couldn't wait to finish. My gaze tracked to the last card. The Death card. Oh, yes, that one. "Um, I'd love to hear what you have to say. Can we skip this card?"

"Come now, this is the most important one. The outcome of your quest. Don't you want to hear the rest of the reading?"

Miranda nudged me with her toe. "C'mon, Lex, do it. What do you have to lose?"

I blinked. She was right. The doctor who diagnosed me, said my cancer was a fast one, but I might have a chance if I started treatment soon. I inhaled, breathing incense into my lungs, along with some courage. "Okay, let's finish this."

Danae nodded and pointed to the last remaining card. "Your outcome is found in the Death card. Remember, there are numerous kinds of endings and many re-births. Some small, and others life-altering. With so many of the Major Arcana cards— the Wheel of Fortune, the Moon, and now Death—that you pulled for this reading, I sense you face massive upheaval and dramatic change."

My gut twisted, coiling around inside like a snake on steroids. "That sounds ominous."

Danae's features softened. "The end result can eclipse your

expectations. Just remember, life is short, so seek real satisfaction and fulfillment while there is still time. Take control of your own destiny and live your life in a meaningful way. Be aware, fear of change is inevitable. Resistance is useless."

"So in other words, do it now while I still can." I tried to hold back the tear, but it slipped over my lash. Before the moisture could track down my cheek, I wiped it away. As I stared at the final card, the woman's alabaster complexion appeared as if death had already kissed her, but the delicate, creamy lily in her hand seemed to point forward to an unknown destination. With my disease, I wouldn't have much of a future. "If only I had money for treatments."

Danae gripped my hand and squeezed my fingers, giving me her support. "Have you ever heard of the blood courtesans?"

Blood courtesans? My mind froze.

Miranda scooted her chair forward, the legs scraping against the wooden floor. "Oh! I think I've heard of them. They, uh, deal with vampires, right?"

Vampires had come out of the woodwork a few decades ago, but I hadn't heard many details about them.

Danae nodded, and a lock of her thick, dark hair fell around her shoulders. "From what I understand, yes. I get all kinds of clients wandering through my business. Let me get you that little something I promised you earlier." She rose from her seat and padded into the kitchen. Her movements were so fluid and sensual, she must be part cat.

Miranda tugged on my arm. "Do you remember Leslie from college? She joined the blood courtesans."

"What do they do?" Curiosity pounded through my veins.

As Danae returned to the room, her soft footfalls pulled me from my thoughts. "I don't know that much about them, but they service vampires."

My heartbeat tripped, part fear, part excitement, which surprised me. "Service them how?"

"Blood, of course, and sex. It's a package deal." Her matter-of-fact tone echoed in the space between us.

Sex? My mouth went dry, tampering the thrill. Other than Allen, my college boyfriend, I didn't have much experience on that front. Besides, I wasn't sure I could afford the loss of blood, but 'beggars can't be choosers,' as my dad used to say. Covering my inexperience, I focused on the latter. "How much blood do they take?"

A crinkle formed between Danae's brows. "Depends on the vampire, I'd imagine, but I can't believe any would take enough to kill you. Blood courtesans are a food source. I doubt they'd bite the hand that feeds them. Well, you know what I mean."

Miranda touched my elbow. "You'll be fine. Just stay away from people with colds. You wouldn't want to catch a bug or get an infection." She wrapped her arms around my shoulders and drew me in for a hug. "Lexi, this could work. I hear they pay a lot."

"I'm not sure they'd take me, with my illness and all."

"Leslie said she's heard that vampires don't get sick like we do." Miranda gave me one of her encouraging smiles. "What could it hurt to at least look into it?"

When I was a kid, I used to wear those plastic Halloween fangs, pulling them out now and then throughout the year to pretend I was a vampire. A coil of anticipation and trepidation churned in my stomach, tightening into a ball. Was it possible? Could I become a blood courtesan?

"Here's a contact number for you. I suggest you don't wait too long." Danae handed me a small business card. Embossed in silver across the gilded paper was the name *'Madame Rouge.'*

I pocketed the card and pushed against the chair's armrests to rise.

"Wait." Danae placed a hand on my shoulder, stopping me. Her eyes flashed an odd shade of yellow, almost like a cat's.

"There's one more tarot card I'd like you to draw, if you have time."

Miranda pulled out her phone and glanced at the screen. "The ferry to Seattle doesn't leave for another hour and our shuttle to Portland is well after that."

My curiosity piqued, I settled into my seat. "All right. What will this card do?"

A soft sigh eased from Danae as she sat. She gripped the deck in her palm, her finger on the top card. "This is a clarification card. It can offer more information and greater details. It may spark new questions or deeper understanding of the energies at work in your life. Now, think about what you wish to know."

I closed my eyes. Dammit. The whole thing reeked of mystery, uncertainty, and misery. I inhaled, long and slow. An unusual peace settled over me, and I opened my eyes to Danae's rich, liquid gaze. "What is my next step?"

She flipped over the card. It was a picture of a man on a throne, a crown around his head, a sphere in his palm. With dark hair, a strong jaw, and aquiline nose, he was handsome except for the grim line of his lips and the sadness in his eyes. I studied the words at the bottom—King of Swords.

"Ah, a very interesting card. He may be a specific person that will fulfill a special role in your journey."

I leaned forward, eagerness tingling my fingers.

"The King of Swords represents wealth. He is a powerful man who may be very opinionated and an authority figure. Perceptive, strong willed, intelligent," Danae stopped for a moment and glanced at me, "his negative qualities can lean toward tyranny and domination. He could be a cruel and cold man."

Our gazes locked. We remained still for several long seconds. Her emotions were well hidden behind her stoic features. I couldn't tell if she worried for me or not.

I broke eye contact and studied the card. "Or it could all be some silly nonsense, right?" Hope made my voice waver, but I didn't think I'd fooled her any more than I'd fooled myself. The card unnerved me.

She gathered up the cards and patted me on the arm. "Call Madame Rouge. I'm sure she can help."

Danae meant well, but that unsettling feeling kept nagging at me.

CHAPTER 2

LEXI

J stood outside Insomniac Coffee and tugged my coat tighter. The green lights of the 'open' sign flashed in the window. Although growing, the vampire population in Portland wasn't large enough to harbor its own recruiter, so I'd had a Skype interview with Madame Rouge from New York.

She'd asked a lot of questions around my sexual experience. There wasn't much to say, having lost my virginity to Allen my sophomore year of college. Although I'd had several boyfriends in high school, he'd been my one and only sexual partner. Even now, the memory of him chatting with a buddy pounded through my mind.

"Lexi is so fucking beautiful, man. She's dull as a box of rocks with all of the bullshit ballerina stuff, but I'm not in it for the conversation." He'd laughed. "I take her out every chance I get, just to let those other douchebags know my game is better than theirs. Doesn't hurt my plays with other chicks either, know what I mean? Side pussy has never been so high quality since I started dating 'beautiful' Lexi."

Now I hate that word…beautiful. That was last year, my senior year at the university. I'd dropped him like yesterday's leftovers and haven't dated since. Maybe that had won me over with Madame Rouge because she'd hired me on the spot then gave me the option of three vampires in the market for a new courtesan, suggesting I sign up with a private Facebook group for blood courtesans in the Portland area that met here. They could answer my questions and help me decide. Although I wanted to meet them, my feet seemed rooted in place.

I exhaled and rubbed the back of my neck. A jolt of pain flared over my shoulders, sending an uncomfortable warmth down my arms. According to the doctors, my tumor was at vertebrae 'T7,' right where my neck met my spine along my shoulders. The mass wasn't big enough to hinder my movements, not yet anyway, but the excruciating pain pushed me to my limits. Steeling my resolve, I yanked open the door and entered the shop.

Voices echoed around the room, the conversations blending into an odd chorus. I searched for anyone who might appear to be a blood courtesan. Not that I knew what one looked like.

Three young women huddled around a nearby table, their laughter adding to the chatter. Nearby, two ladies in their early thirties sipped coffee and studied their phones. At the back of the room, four others sat in some easy chairs, deep in conversation. Like a trip-hammer, my heart pounded. Any of them could be blood courtesans.

"Are you Lexi?" A pretty girl with short brown hair and a pixie nose strode toward me, steam rising from the cup of coffee in her hand. On her shoulder, the line of a tribal tattoo peeked from beneath her tight-fitting cashmere sweater.

A knot formed between my shoulders. "That's me."

Her smile widened. "Perfect. I'm Josie from the Facebook group. C'mon, join us."

She gripped my arm and drew me toward the laughing young

women. One had short curly hair and dark skin. Another was small in frame with Asian features. The third had red hair and freckles. Despite their differences, they were all attractive.

Josie cleared her throat. "Lexi, this is Simone, Kiko, and Briana. Ladies, we have a new member. Say 'hi' to Lexi."

A chorus of hellos erupted from the women. Kiko stood and wrapped me in a warm embrace. The tension in my shoulders eased, and I smiled at their heartfelt welcome.

Josie tugged on my arm. "How do you like your coffee?"

"Oh, you don't have to do that—"

"I insist. It's the least I can do for a new courtesan. Now, what kind?"

I exhaled, but I couldn't resist the offer. "Thank you. Black, please."

"I'm on it." Josie snapped her fingers and headed for the counter.

Kiko pulled out a chair, offering it to me.

I gave her a quick nod in thanks and sat.

She tsked, the sound warm and full of reverence. "My, my, you're a looker."

Simone winked, a strand of her dark hair catching in her eyelash. "You'll make a wonderful blood courtesan. With your blonde hair, blue eyes, and fair skin, the vampires will fight over you. You're stunningly beautiful."

She'd said the awful word, and deep inside, I wanted to scream. Instead, my cheeks heated. "I'm not sure what to say."

Briana giggled, and her green eyes sparked, accentuating her freckles. "I think the vamps will love how her face flushes, don't you?"

"Oh, indeed." Kiko gripped my fingers and leaned close. "Blushing is very erotic. The rush of blood under the skin. Vampires love that."

"Don't forget about the sex." Simone tapped her long fingernail against her mug. "The physical act enhances the flavor of

13

blood, fills it with good endorphins. That drives the vamps crazy."

A strange sense of unease rippled over my skin followed by a curiosity that surprised me. My experiences with Allen had left me longing for something I couldn't name. If only I could trust a man with my heart. I shook the thought from my brain. I was here to learn about the job, 'job' being the key word.

I blurted the question burning at the back of my mind before I'd thought better of it. "Does it hurt?"

"The bite or the sex?" Josie handed me a mug, the dark liquid looking eerily similar to blood. She sat in the open chair next to me. Her evaluating gaze roamed my face, yet her eyes radiated warmth.

I took a sip, using the drink as a distraction. The hot liquid burned my throat. "Both," I choked.

Josie shrugged. "Well, being bitten outside of intercourse can be painful, but sex with a vampire will blow…you…away. I guarantee it will be the best sex you've ever had and probably ruin you for life. Also, you don't have to worry about getting pregnant or catching an STD from a vampire."

A spark of anticipation swelled in my chest, but given my circumstances, I wasn't sure I'd survive even if I had the treatments. This might be my only opportunity to experience great sex. The idea settled over me. Might as well go out with a bang. "What makes the sex so good?"

Josie glanced between the other three women before her gaze returned to mine. A twinkle glinted in her eyes. "Some things are better left to discover on your own."

I sighed, my shoulders slumping. "Naturally. So, why do vampires use courtesans?"

Kiko raised her hand. "I had to ask that one, too. I'm pretty new myself, needed the money to pay off some family debt. Most vampires prefer fresh blood to blood-fortified wine and many don't want a long-term commitment. When they get tired of a courtesan, they get a new one. So, my advice, keep your relationship at a business level."

"Madame gave me the option of three vampires looking for a new courtesan—Chase, William, or Gavin. She said you might be able to help me choose."

Briana sniffed. "Do yourself a favor. Stay away from Gavin. You're better off with either Chase or William."

I tensed. Trepidation skipped down my back, triggering a ripple of pain that reverberated from my spine into my chest. I furrowed my brow as much in confusion as to hide my discomfort. "Why not Gavin?"

Simone, Kiko, and Briana all jumped in at once.

"He never takes you to his bed. If he screws you, and that's a big if, it's always someplace else."

"I've heard he's a monster under that mask. He scares me."

"He never goes outside, but no one knows why. It's kind of creepy."

Josie raised her hand, silencing the others. "Despite what we may think of Gavin Morris, he's the most generous. If you can endure becoming his courtesan, he pays enough that you never have to work again."

I swallowed. "Is he really that awful?"

The chilling look that passed between the courtesans said it all. Indeed, he was.

Briana drew her hand through her hair, tucking a few stray strands behind her ear. "When does Madame Rouge want your answer?"

"Tomorrow."

Josie gripped my fingers and gave them a squeeze. "Do what you must, but choose wisely."

"Thank you," I whispered. Despite my misgivings, a small flicker of hope flared. *Maybe, just maybe, things would work out.*

CHAPTER 3

LEXI

*T*he limousine lurched forward, and I banged my head against the window. Pain blossomed at my temple, but I bit my tongue to keep the short cry from escaping my lips. Max, the driver, had been evaluating me through the rearview mirror since the moment he picked me up. The last thing I wanted was to appear weak.

Feigning an itch, I brushed my fingers along my hairline, rubbing at the sore spot. I breathed deep and that new car smell, a mixture of leather, clean carpeting, and who knows what else, eased into my senses. If my father hadn't envied expensive, classy cars, I never would've recognized *The Spirit of Ecstasy* hood ornament on the front of the Rolls Royce when the car rolled up in front of my apartment building. Only the superrich could afford such luxury.

Through the tinted windows, moonlight piercing between the tree branches cast eerie shadows over the pavement. The pointed tips resembled fangs, reminding me of my destination. Soon, I'd meet Gavin Morris, vampire.

My pulse rose with as much anticipation as trepidation.

"Are you comfortable?" Max's low voice traveled through the car's interior space.

I glanced to the rearview mirror. Although I couldn't see his eyes, I sensed his gaze on me. Goosebumps rose along my arms, and I longed for the coat I'd left at my apartment. Late October in Portland could be tricky, sometimes warm, sometimes cool. It was always a gamble. The thin chemise blouse and short tight-fitting skirt that covered very little of my curves were part of the wardrobe requirement.

"Less is more." Madame Rouge's words filtered through my mind.

I rubbed my arms, easing away some of the chill, then placed my hands in my lap. He didn't need to see my discomfort. "I'm fine, thank you."

He nodded. "If you're thirsty, there's water, wine, and other spirits in the cabinet. We'll arrive at the mansion in a few minutes."

Anxiety kept me rooted in place. With my luck, I'd spill my drink on the seat. My thoughts returned to Madame Rouge and the choices I'd made today.

Gavin Morris.

I repeated his name in my mind. It had a nice ring to it, but the hair at my nape prickled anyway. The comments from the other courtesans had left me with a sense of unease. Maybe I was a fool, but I'd signed the contract for an initial meeting—more 'to be determined.'

Gavin lived on the outskirts of Portland, in a secluded, wooded area far from the hustle and bustle of the city. According to Josie, his only friends were Max, his driver, and Ester, his housekeeper.

My mouth felt like I'd eaten some cotton balls, all dry and sticky. The water Max offered took on a new appeal. I yanked open the cabinet and drew out a cold plastic bottle. As I twisted the lid, the crackle penetrated throughout the cab. With shaky hands, I brought the bottle to my mouth. The cool liquid slipped past my lips.

Max chuckled. "Glad you decided to have a drink. A dehydrated courtesan won't do."

My throat constricted even as my insides fluttered. *"I guarantee it will be the best sex you've ever had and probably ruin you for life."* Josie's words tripped through my mind. She'd seemed so confident. I wasn't sure what to expect, but I'd travelled down the road this far, I refused to turn around.

Curiosity about the vampire I was about to meet bolstered my courage. "Max, what's Gavin like?"

The muscles in Max's shoulders tensed. "Courtesans don't ask about their clients."

"Why not?"

Although I couldn't see it, I felt his gaze on me. "It prevents confusion and false impressions."

"I'd think it would clear that up instead, unless Gavin has something to hide."

Max exhaled. "Gavin hasn't had an easy time and is often misunderstood. Don't judge him too harshly."

A sudden coldness hit me in the chest. My mind spun. Gavin, the vampire, had once been human, with dreams, desires, goals. *He's as real as I am.*

The car slowed. As it crested a small hill, lights from an elaborate mansion spilled from the front porch and a single window on the third floor. The remaining dark windows seemed empty of life.

The goosebumps reformed, spreading up my arms in an instant.

A few moments later, the car stopped in front of the cobblestone entryway. Max killed the engine and stepped out of the limo. The door shut with a soft click. Silence filled the small space.

A feeling of entrapment prickled my scalp. Why had I agreed to become a blood courtesan? Well, I needed the money so I could begin my treatments. That's why.

The sooner I started the better my chances of beating the cancer. I fisted my hand, my fingernails cutting into my skin. Hope, based on a thin possibility, fueled my resolve. I wanted to fulfill my dream to dance on a live stage, and I'd do whatever it took to increase my odds.

My door opened, and the chilly night air wrapped around me like a cloak. Instead of finding comfort in the feeling, I shivered.

"Welcome to the Morris estate." Max held out his hand, a gesture for me to exit my little safe haven.

Pulling on my inner determination, I clamped my jaw and slipped my fingers into his proffered palm. With a gentle tug, he eased me from the car.

Bathed in shadow from the house lights, I couldn't see his features. Tall with broad shoulders, *linebacker* didn't quite cover his description, but the formal suit he wore seemed at odds with his build. Before I could thank him, he released my hand and headed toward the front door. "This way please."

I slid my fingers down my skirt, smoothing out the wrinkles and attempting to push the material further down my thigh. The breeze picked up, slipping through my thin chemise. My nipples hardened. Even in the dark, I could tell the little round nubs protruded against the material. My cheeks heated.

The mansion's front entry overshadowed much of the space. Up close, its brick exterior spoke of wealth and influence from a bygone era. Cracks ran through some of the bricks, giving the place a frightening appearance. Even the welcome mat, with its etched gothic scrollwork, seemed spooky, yet the gorgeous mahogany doors gleamed in the light. Such a contradiction.

The click of a lock disengaging echoed. Light from the interior flooded the entryway.

Max stepped aside. Bathed in illumination, I caught a glimpse of his appearance for the first time. Tall with blond hair and blue eyes, his Nordic features and strong build brought images of masculine Vikings to the forefront of my mind. He didn't seem much older than my twenty-two years, but the wisdom in his gaze made him seem much older. Was he a vampire? "Please enter. First door on your right you'll find the library. Gavin will be waiting for you there."

"You're not coming in?" Stall tactic, but I couldn't help myself.

A smirk formed on his lips, revealing a glint of a fang and answering my earlier question. "Tonight, you are his guest. I'll wait in the car. When you are ready to leave, come outside. I'll take you home."

I swallowed and turned my attention to the hallway. Light from the single chandelier traveled only so far but lit the outline of a doorway on my right. I raised my chin and forced my feet to step over the doorsill.

"Each journey begins with a single step." My father's words echoed in my mind. He'd always encouraged me to try new things. I couldn't imagine what he'd think of my situation.

As I stepped forward, my high heels clicked against the expensive, high-quality wooden floor. I clutched my small purse, my nails digging into the soft material. Vibrant with color, exquisite landscape paintings lined the walls. A grandfather clock, dark grain polished to a exceptional sheen, stood next to an antique desk. Glass figurines, reminiscent of pieces I'd seen in a trip to the Louvre with my dad, lined the top.

Rumors were Gavin made his money in real estate and the stock market. Seemed he liked antiques. Although priceless, I didn't care for old furniture. The place seemed like something my great-grandmother would've liked.

The door clicked softly behind me. Max was gone. I was alone in the mansion with Gavin.

My heart beat double time. Madame Rouge indicated vampires had extra special senses and used scent to evaluate compatibility. He could probably hear me and smell my fear in the sweat at the back of my neck. *Great, just great.*

I reached the door and wrapped my fingers around the cool metal handle, but I didn't open it. The courtesans' troubling comments loomed in my mind, preying on my insecurities. Could Gavin really be dark and dangerous?

I twisted the knob and pushed open the door.

Gaudy elegance like I'd never seen before made me blink. A large expanse of wooden tile lined the floor, gleaming in the light from the ornate crystal chandelier. Books stacked in elegant bookcases lined the walls. A fire crackled in the hearth, and the warmth filtered over my skin.

Except for a coat rack, a gilded antique music stand, a violin nestled in its case, and a single wingback chair with a small end table, the large room was void of furniture. With all the money he had, he could afford anything, yet he kept it sparse.

Bathed in the light from the fireplace, the chair's shadow danced over the polished wooden floor, almost enticing me to do the same. I imagined myself twirling in my ballet shoes, enjoying the expansive space.

Gavin was nowhere to be seen. Uncertainty toyed with me, and I took a step back. The door behind me closed with a soft click.

"Alexandra Dixon."

I jumped at the deep, rumbling male voice.

My attention focused on the wingback furniture. A pair of dress shoes became visible under the seat. My finger tapped against my purse in quick succession, as if it had a mind of its own. I took a deep breath and forced myself to remain still. "Please, call me Lexi."

He chuckled, the sound low and controlled. "Your given name rolls off the tongue in such an enchanting way. I shall call you Alexandra. There's a bar on the back wall. Pour yourself something. Spiked lemonade perhaps. I like the contrast of the bitterness with the sweet."

My stomach flipped and fluttered like a bunch of moths had found their way in. "Th…thank you."

Calm down, Lexi. Don't let him see you sweat. With as much dignity as possible, I made my way to the stunning carved bar in the far corner of the room.

I hadn't noticed the glossy wooden beams before, but someone had taken great pride in maintaining its appearance. Glasses, bottles of wine, and expensive liqueurs of all different shapes and sizes lined the shelves, lit by hidden lightbulbs within the wood. A large pitcher filled with lemonade sat on the counter, sliced lemons swimming in the liquid.

I set my purse on the bar and wrapped my trembling fingers around one of the glasses. A bejeweled wine charm clinked against the stem, but through sheer force of will I steadied the goblet. As I poured the liquid, a few lemon slices slid into the cup along with several ice cubes. I took a sip of my drink. The back of my throat burned, and my eyes watered. I pinched my mouth shut.

"You're a brave girl coming to see the reclusive and vile Gavin Morris. Not many courtesans will make the trip."

I raised my chin. "I don't believe everything I hear."

He chuckled. "That's good, very good indeed. Come here."

I set down my glass and took a step forward then another, curiosity pushing me onward. Perhaps he'd compelled me. I wasn't sure. Visible over the chair's back, his hair, shiny and black, reflected the fire's glow.

Clothes rustled. The chair groaned.

Gavin stood and turned to face me.

My heart stuttered. He was at least 6' 5", with broad shoulders and a muscular build. Dressed in a tailored suit, his dark hair hung below his chin, the silky strands teasing the collar. Backlit by the fire with half his face shrouded in darkness, only the left side was visible. A silver mask covered part of his forehead, left eye, and cheek with a string trailing under his ear. The fine etched metal seemed to shift colors from orange to deep red in tandem with the fluctuating flames, enticing and chilling at the same time.

I inhaled, the sound loud in the enclosed space.

He angled himself so the fire lit up the right side of his face. His delectable plump lips thinned, sadness reflected in his deep brown eye, and his shoulders stiffened. "Your reaction is as I expected, but no matter. I hired you for a job. Let's begin, shall we?"

Despite the mask, Gavin was handsome in a way I couldn't describe, and he reminded me of the last tarot card, the King of Swords. Would he be cruel and cold as the card foretold?

CHAPTER 4

LEXI

I bit my lip, tugging at the fleshy part with my teeth. Gavin's good eye narrowed on my mouth. Red flickered through his iris. The warmth of the fire had chased away my chill long ago and now it seemed as hot as a roaring furnace in here. Sweat beaded between my breasts and slid down my skin.

"You want to start? Like drink from me already?" The words slipped from my mouth before I could stop them. Regret made me cringe.

Gavin raised his eyebrow. "That's what you're here for, isn't it? For the money?"

I swallowed. He was right. That was exactly why I was here.

As I took in his overpowering presence, his shoulders stiffened, bunching beneath his tailored suit. He twirled a gold ring around the middle finger on his right hand, the jewelry catching the fire's light and reflecting across the floor.

I drew on my courage, the cost of my treatment urging me on.

"You're right, I need the money, but please understand, I've never done this before."

"Come closer." His deep masculine voice, sexy as sin, wound around me and worked its way under my skin. It was a siren song all its own.

I forced a smile and stepped into his personal space. His unique scent, like black licorice and spices, filtered into my senses, reeling me in. A part of me wanted to lick him, see if he tasted as good as he smelled. I gasped at the errant thought, and a flutter, unexpected and quick, tickled me deep inside.

As if he had every right, he placed his hand around the back of my neck and cradled my head in his palm. Wrapping his other arm around my waist, he tugged me close.

I cried out. My palms landed on his pecs. Even through his silky button-down shirt, the firm plane of his muscles was rock hard beneath my fingertips. Desire flared in my chest.

He chuckled and dipped his face to my throat. An involuntary shiver, a mixture of fear and yearning, rippled down my arms. With a tenderness I'd only ever dreamed about, he kissed me on the neck, right below the ear. Electrified heat raced all the way to my core, causing a rush of wetness to dampen my panties.

I expected him to inhale, smell my desire as well as our compatibility, but he didn't. Instead, he pressed his lips against my jugular vein.

My pulse quickened.

His breath, warm and enticing, tickled my skin.

I closed my eyes and waited for his bite.

To my surprise, he drew away and trailed a finger down the side of my face.

I cracked open my eyelids and peered at him.

A knowing grin, part amusement, part skepticism tugged at his mouth. One fang protruded over his bottom lip and glistened in the firelight. "Alexandra, you are so very beautiful."

I stiffened. *Beautiful.* The hateful word again. Why was that all a man ever saw of me?

Gavin relaxed his grip, letting me go. Before I knew it, he stood by the large picture window, arms crossed, staring into the night. He'd moved so fast I couldn't track him. "If you don't wish to perform your duties, you are free to leave. Have Max take you home."

I gaped at him. It wasn't Gavin that made me cringe, it was years of conditioning from my high school classmates to be just what my old boyfriend Allen had expected me to be—obedient, docile, and beautiful. The first two I battled on a daily basis. The last, well, I wasn't up for scarring myself.

Gavin glanced at me. Red, the color of hot coals, burned in his eye so intently it glowed.

My nervousness returned, worming its way into my gut. Other courtesans feared Gavin. Maybe I should as well. Yet, there was something about him, the sadness in his eye perhaps, that called to me.

I exhaled and wiped my hands down my short skirt, pretending to straighten the tight material. "If you're giving me a choice, I'd rather stay. It's just...I don't like being called 'beautiful'."

A low chuckle eased from him. "Perhaps it's my job to teach you to love that word."

I looked for a distraction. The violin nestled in its open case beckoned to me, so I wandered over to it. Elegant detail in the wood's exquisite grain showed signs of wear, yet the polished piece spoke of great care. I focused on a small label, visible through the f-shaped tone hole. *Antonius Stradivarius Cremonensis Faciebot Anno 1697.* The first numeral was typed, but the rest were hand written.

I swallowed. Along with ballet, my father was an avid orchestra lover. He'd told me about Stradivarius violins and how you could tell an authentic one from a fake. With the hand-written numerals, this was the real deal. I trailed my fingers over the strings and glanced at Gavin. "Would you play this for—"

In an instant, he was on me, gripping my hips and pushing me backward until my bottom hit the wall. He captured my wrists in his fingers and pinned them over my head. When his forearms connected with the surface, the wood shuddered under the impact. He pressed his large chest against mine, trapping me with one knee between my legs.

I struggled against him, his body as immovable as granite. He could have hurt me in an instant, but hadn't. Instead, his embrace was gentle. I stopped my struggles and relaxed. My focus drew to his mask. The silver facade, fine lines etched in a scroll-like pattern, displayed the craftsman's attention to detail.

Gavin's luscious full mouth, mere inches from mine, pursed. He studied me, his attention flicking over my features. I licked my lips. His intense gaze darted there for a long moment before returning to my eyes.

My insides melted at what I saw reflected there—desire, anticipation, need.

"Don't touch the Stradivarius." His cool, minty breath eased over my cheeks, tickling my skin.

Confusion wracked my brain, stalling my thoughts. "What?"

He smiled, and this close, I got a good look at his fangs. Long and pointed, they were nothing like the plastic pair I used to play with as a child.

He dropped his head to my neck, his lips trailing over my jugular once again. "I said, don't touch the Stradivarius."

"Why not?" My breaths, short and quick, eased from my mouth.

"Over the last one hundred and twenty years, only my hands have touched that violin." He grazed his tooth along my neck, pricking at me.

27

120 years... "How old are you?"

"I was born January 14ᵗʰ, 1879."

"So that makes you one hundred and thirty-nine."

"Very good. Smart as well as...beautiful." He chuckled, and the vibration travelled along my nerves, lighting up my senses.

I gasped as much from his touch as from the hateful word he said even after I'd told him how much I despised it.

With his free hand, he trailed his finger down my rib cage and over my hip. The movement was sensual, possessive, and I couldn't stop the slow moan as it eased from my lips.

He pressed his knee harder against the wall, pushing up my skirt and encouraging me to spread my legs.

With a soft whimper, I complied.

"And, my spunky Alexandra, how young are you?" Gavin slid his fingers along my thigh until he reached the juncture between my legs.

"Twenty-two."

"Ah, the perfect age." He brushed his fingers over my panties, circling the outer edges of my mound. My body responded, my nipples peaking under the sheer top.

A groan eased from Gavin's lips, and he rubbed his chest against mine, teasing the hard nubs. His one eye, vibrant red, stared at me.

Caught like a fly in a web, I couldn't look away. "The perfect age for what?"

"For sex, of course. Dearest Alexandra," he slipped one finger under the edge of my lace panties, "tell me, how many men have you slept with?"

"Just one." Heat raced up my throat and into my face.

Gavin's gaze riveted on my cheek then slid to my neck. "You have the prettiest, most alluring skin, especially when you blush. I must say, pink is my new favorite color, at least on you."

He slipped his finger between my slit and circled the wet folds, skimming closer to my sensitive bud with each turn.

My legs shook. His touch, his scent, his voice weakened me. I'd spun down a hole and couldn't seem to stop. I wasn't sure I wanted to.

At last, his finger brushed over my already hard and waiting clit. He circled it again, and my hips gyrated, matching his rhythm stroke for stroke. Relentless and unforgiving, he increased the pace, lowering his head to my neck, kissing my skin.

As his finger grazed my hard little nub one last time, a rush of desire exploded inside. With my hands still bound by him, the sensation deepened, and I bucked against him.

A sharp pinprick of pain flared below my ear as his teeth breached my skin and sank into my flesh. I flinched, but my orgasm had me in its grasp, and all I could do was ride the wave.

As the last of my shudders rippled through me, Gavin licked my neck, sealing the wound. My skin pulsed at the site, uncomfortable and hot. A wave of dizziness crested over me. White spots formed in my vision.

"Stay with me." Gavin released my wrists, and my arms fell limp to my sides. He swiped his arm under my legs, lifted me up, and cradled me against his broad chest.

I concentrated on breathing, but the flaming ache along my neck blazed like I'd been stung by a hundred angry bees. "Why did you do that?"

"Do what?" He placed me in the lone chair next to the fire. The warmth from the flames was not what I wanted right now. It aggravated the throbbing ache.

"I'd heard vampires bite during sex to ease the pain. You didn't have sex with me." The fog in my brain started to clear. I realized what I'd said. Heat from my embarrassment tinged my cheeks.

"Alexandra, there are no absolutes when it comes to vampires or courtesans. Everyone has a different pain tolerance. For some, sex enhances the experience, while others experience discomfort.

The orgasm is usually sufficient, but," Gavin placed a cool glass in my hand, "drink this. It's a special concoction of mine. It will help ease the pain, and don't worry, after you flinched, I didn't drink from you."

I brought the glass to my lips and gulped the clear liquid. It was all I could do to keep the goblet from slipping from my grasp. The pain in my neck eased, but a slight soreness still pulsed with each heartbeat.

"Why didn't you want to..." I didn't need to finish my question, the answer ripping through my mind. *He didn't want me.* A bitter taste formed in my mouth, his rejection stinging far worse than his bite.

His attention wandered over my thin blouse then down my short skirt before meeting my gaze. "Over the years I've become very adept at reading people. You're hiding something from me, Alexandra. What is it?"

I blinked, my mind racing through possibilities. "I don't know what you're talking about."

A tic pulsed to life in his jaw, accentuating a small dimple that formed in his cheek. It was adorable.

His focus narrowed. "You said you've only been with one man. I don't believe you. If I chose to do so, I could use compulsion to obtain my answer, but I won't. I know why you're here. Curiosity." He placed his hands on the wingback's arms, caging me in. "Would you like to see what's behind the mask?" He sneered.

I dug my fingernails into the chair's arm. "That's not why I'm here, and I didn't lie to you. I've only ever been with Allen."

"Allen, such a normal name, but why should I believe you? You're a courtesan, the very definition of a whore, and far too...beautiful."

Before I could think about my reaction, my palm connected with the skin on his good check. The slap echoed in the space between us.

"I'm neither a liar nor a whore." I spat the words at him, and a drop of my saliva landed on his chin.

With a quick push, he stood and wiped the moisture away with the back of his hand. The flames flared in the fire, sparking and popping as if in anger. "Go, leave now."

I jumped from the chair and darted across the room, the heels of my shoes clicking against the polished floor. My purse, sitting on the bar, caught my attention, so I detoured to it before reaching the door. As I wrapped my fingers around the knob, my chest ached. I wasn't sure why.

"Alexandra, one week." Gavin's low voice stopped me cold.

I tensed, but didn't turn around. "What?"

"Return to me in one week. As an incentive, I'll double the payment."

Hell no would I see him again. The pain between my shoulders had to be better than putting up with this vampire for one more moment. I inhaled, the words on the tip of my tongue, but when I turned toward him, sadness etched lines around his eye.

My heartbeat stuttered for a moment. A groundswell of empathy surged in my chest, and the memory of his scent, his touch, his voice took my breath away. The words I'd wanted to say died on my lips.

Instead, I swallowed several times, clearing my throat. When I could speak, my words came out in a rush. "I'll think about it."

He nodded once, his eye flickering with red, but a small smile tugged at his lips. He knew as well as I that I'd come back. If for no other reason, I needed the money. One payment wouldn't cover all my treatments, but a double one would surely get me a long way. That was the real reason I'd return, and I walked out the door with my chin held high.

~

GAVIN

A hard knot lodged itself in my gut, twisting my insides. Alexandra Dixon, a blood courtesan, had stood up to me, even slapping me across the cheek for my insolence. That was a first. Most of the courtesans feared me, which was by design, a necessity to protect them from the monster inside.

I stared at Alexandra through the library's window. Her graceful dancer's hips swayed as she strode toward the Rolls. Soft and blonde, the color of golden wheat, her hair bounced against her blouse. With her gorgeous sea-blue eyes, high cheekbones, and beautiful skin, she'd captivated me from the start.

Max let her in, and as she yanked on the handle, the slam of the door echoed against the mansion's brick.

I smiled, and that was something I didn't do often. This young woman intrigued me. I shouldn't have asked her to return. With my history, I might hurt her—or worse.

But something about her had soothed my inner demon.

A vision of Lorraine tugged at my memory, but I shut it down before the nightmare rose to the surface. I stroked my index finger over the mask's scrollwork, the intricate design rough against my fingertip. After all these years, the bitterness still burned along the scars. Curling my hand into a fist, I fought the revulsion rising in my throat. *Damn you, Lorraine.*

With Alexandra, I'd have to be careful. I couldn't afford to let her get too close. Her life, as well as my sanity, depended upon it. Yet, I couldn't let her walk away.

The Roll's engine roared to life, and a moment later, the limo eased down the driveway. When the taillights disappeared over the hill, I pushed away from the window and strode to my Stradivarius. I cradled the instrument against my chin, closed my eyes, and stroked the bow across the strings, losing myself in the only thing that brought me any comfort and ignoring the growing realization that perhaps, after tonight, there were two things in the world that could soothe me.

CHAPTER 5

LEXI

The autumn morning sunshine snuck past the grime on the window in my second-story apartment. Golden-hued, the ray shone across the kitchen table and lit up my bowl of Wheaties. I usually woke at seven a.m., but I'd overslept, too tired to drag myself out of bed. What finally got me moving was the needle-like pain racing down my right arm and numbing my hand.

With the doctors' appointments and all the medical tests and treatments, the week had passed faster than I'd thought possible. Exhaustion aggravated the ache in my back, but much of that was due to my illness, not the hectic schedule. One thing I had to look forward to with radiation was loss of hair at the treatment site. The doctors warned me I could receive a bald spot on the back of my head or even a bit more. Perfect. Add insult to injury.

Thank God I'd quit my job at Hooties. The constant ogling by the men was more than I could take. If I only had a few months left, I didn't want to spend it there with a bunch of horny dudes. I wiped the dribble of milk from my chin and peered at my father's picture on the wall above the cuckoo clock.

Although the gray at his temple showed his age, his eyes gleamed with happiness. A small trout dangled from the fishing pole in his hand. His other arm, wrapped around my shoulders, brought back a ghost of his embrace, warm and tender. My chest ached. Since he'd passed, a permanent loneliness had invaded my heart, one I couldn't seem to fill. "Hey, Dad, miss you."

I slid from my chair, grabbed my empty bowl and spoon, and headed for the sink. The bright sunlight blinded me, and the dish slipped from my fingers. The bowl connected with its destiny, the ceramic shards scattering across the floor.

I sighed. Just one more thing to do.

I tossed the spoon into the sink and grabbed some paper towels. As I picked up a little blue shard, the sharp edge nicked my finger. Blood welled in the cut. I stuck the appendage into my mouth. A salty taste assailed my senses.

What was it vampires found so appealing about blood? Would Gavin find mine pleasurable? My pulse quickened. *"You're a courtesan, the very definition of a whore, and far too...beautiful."* Despite his hurtful words, when he'd pushed me against the hard wall, he'd cradled me in his embrace. A contradiction, for sure, and he'd intrigued me. Maybe that's why I'd agreed to see him again and signed another one-time contract.

I shook my head, picked up the last of the bowl's remains, and tossed them into the trash. My gaze tracked to the dark marks, almost like bruises, and the blistery bumps on the back of my arm, new additions as of yesterday, and a reaction to my treatment. At least the money Gavin deposited in my bank account had been enough to start radiation. My next treatment —tomorrow.

The cuckoo clock burst into its familiar melody. As the bird chirped, I counted. *One, two, three, four, five, six, seven, eight, nine, ten.* "Ten a.m.," I muttered. "Nine more hours until Max picks me up."

I touched my neck. Despite the initial pain, the wound had healed in a couple of days, leaving only a small mark. I frowned. If I hadn't remembered every detail in great clarity, I almost could've convinced myself it hadn't happened. Would Gavin bite me in the same spot or someplace new? Would it hurt?

I'd already received Gavin's payment and tonight I'd have even more. Twice the usual fee. I could handle a little pain.

My phone beeped. I darted to the kitchen table and picked it up. The number was unknown to me. With a quick finger swipe across the screen, I answered. "Hello?"

"Is this Alexandra Dixon?" a woman's cheerful voice asked.

"Yes."

"My name is Rachel Warfield from the Oregon Ballet Theater. You auditioned with us a few months ago. I'm calling you because we've had a couple of dancers leave us for personal reasons, and I wondered if you'd be interested in coming in for another audition."

My heart skipped a beat then picked up its pace. This was what I'd waited for my entire life. The chance to dance ballet with a professional theater troupe. I opened my mouth to say 'yes, yes, yes,' but hesitated. I could still dance, but who knew for how much longer? It wouldn't be fair to take a spot when I wouldn't be able to perform because of my illness. My exuberance deflated like a flat ball.

"Hello? Miss Dixon?"

I exhaled the breath I didn't realize I'd held. "I'm here. This is just so unexpected."

"Well, to be honest, the position would be as a backup, a temporary job. You'd mostly be around to help the others and sub in if something happens."

"Oh." My gaze flicked to my father's picture. My number one supporter, he'd attended all of my performances, every last one.

"Keep trying, kiddo, you never know when you'll catch your big break." His words of encouragement bubbled to the surface.

My gut tightened, resolve forming deep inside. I wanted to perform, dance for my father's memory as well as for myself. If they offered me the position and I couldn't dance, I'd turn it down. "Ms. Warfield. I'd love to try out. When is the audition?"

"Well…," she exhaled loud enough the sound carried over the line, "here's the thing. We have some time this afternoon. Could you be here by one?"

I stared at the cuckoo clock, my mind racing through today's timeline. If I hurried, I could do the audition and make it back here in time to meet Max. I expelled a relieved breath. "I'll be there."

"Ooh, so glad to hear that. We look forward to your performance. See you then."

"Thank you." I clutched the phone to my chest and twirled around the small space, careful to avoid the rickety chair. Feather light, my lungs expanded, the rush of air filling me with a happiness I hadn't known since before my father died.

My phone buzzed. A text message, probably just a confirmation of the audition date and time. I glanced at the screen.

"You will receive a package with something silky and comfortable inside. Wear it tonight. I look forward to seeing you in my selection." The unlisted caller ID blinked on my screen, but I knew who the text was from.

My stomach somersaulted, a mixture of delight, eagerness, and unease curling into a giant knot. This day would be one to remember.

CHAPTER 6

LEXI

*T*he ride in Gavin's Rolls Royce seemed much faster than last time or maybe I was preoccupied. My day had been a whirlwind. I ran my fingers over the smooth silk dress and admired how the little blue sequins shimmered, even under the car dome's muted interior light.

The dress wasn't quite what I'd expected, not from a vampire to a courtesan, anyway. Short, about halfway up my thigh, the material was elegant despite its skimpy appearance. One shoulder was bare, but the sleeve on the other side flowed to my wrist, covering up my radiation burns and latest bruise. Skin tight, the neckline plunged deep into my cleavage. By design, a bra was out of the question.

A single hand-written note had accompanied the package. *"Panties are an unnecessary distraction."*

A little shiver of anticipation ran over my bare shoulder just like it had when I'd first read the words. Naughty as it was, I'd done as he'd instructed.

The car turned down the drive, and the brick mansion came into view. The image wasn't as scary as last time. Instead, a sadness radiated from the place, maybe in part due to the cracks in a few of the bricks and the broken shingles on the roof. My recollection of the interior's well-maintained space was in stark contrast, much like the owner.

"We're here, Lexi." Max peered at me through the rearview mirror. "I'll be around in a moment to let you out."

I nodded. If Max wanted to be a gentleman, who was I to complain?

The door whooshed open, and the cool night air wafted over my exposed skin. As before, the single light next to the rich mahogany door greeted me.

Max extended his palm, and I took it, exiting the car, careful not to let the girls slip from the material. My worries were for nothing, though. The sequined dress fell into place, quality all the way.

"Did you forget something?" Max pointed to my vacated seat.

My handbag lay on the cushion. The light brown faux leather didn't match my outfit, in quality or style, but it was all I had. "Is it all right if I leave my purse there?"

He nodded and gave me a wink. "It'll be waiting for you when we leave."

As I stepped inside the front door, the soft melody of a violin floated across the entryway. My breath caught in my throat. I glanced around the foyer for Gavin.

"We're a bit early. Please wait outside the library until he's through." Max placed his large palm on the door, opening it further.

"Thank you." I strode toward the room I'd visited last time. The closer I approached, the music grew louder, and I could discern the piece, a refrain from *Swan Lake*. I inhaled, my lungs expanding with happiness. *Swan Lake* was my favorite ballet.

Growing up, I'd often danced to this song for my father in our home.

A shaft of light penetrated through the small crack in the doorway. Max's words to stay outside flicked through my brain, but I ignored them. Placing my fingers against the wood, I gave the door a slight push. It slid open without a sound.

Dressed in an elegant dark suit, Gavin stood next to the music stand, the sheet paper scattered along the rim. He cradled the violin under his chin, his mask almost touching the instrument's wooden belly. The fingers on his left hand pressed the strings against the fingerboard, and he stroked the bow over the taut strands with such passion, it was as if the instrument were a lover in his embrace.

My stomach fluttered, and for a moment, I wanted him to show me that kind of attention, not as a courtesan, not for my beauty or my blood, but for who I was on the inside.

He didn't seem to notice me, so I stepped closer. Mesmerized by the melody, I slipped from my high-heeled shoes. I skimmed across the floor, and I pirouetted, following the rhythm of my favorite opus as I had long ago. I closed my eyes, letting the hum of the bow over the strings work its magic. Joy filled me as I forgot everything except the music and the pleasure of dancing.

The music stopped.

I halted.

An echo from the last chord rebounded against the wall.

My gaze flicked to Gavin.

He held the bow in mid-air, the violin still cradled under his chin. His attention riveted on me. "What are you doing here?"

My mouth went dry. "I…we…had an appointment."

With deliberate intent, his gaze slid from my eyes to my breasts, lingering there before continuing over my hips and down my thighs. Heat radiated across the space between us. When at last he returned his focus to my face, his eye glowed a deep shade of red. "Didn't Max tell you to wait outside?"

I took a cautious step forward. "You're very talented. Why can't I listen?"

A soft growl rose from his throat, and he slammed the folder shut, the music stand shuddering from the impact. He didn't look at me, but placed the Stradivarius into its case. "I prefer to be alone. You're here to service me. Don't..." Wiping his mouth with the back of his hand, his shoulders tensed.

"Don't judge him too harshly." Max's words filtered through my brain.

I strode toward Gavin, the wooden floor cool against my bare feet. Without my heels, I was much shorter than him. Even still, I didn't fear Gavin, not really. Instead, I trailed my finger over his shoulder and down his arm, encouraging him to look at me.

When he turned, I spoke before he could get a word in, the words tumbling from my lips. "My father used to play that song for me on our CD player when I was a kid, over and over again. I'd dance and dance and dance. That song, and his encouragement, is what made me pursue ballet as a career." Tears welled in my eyes, and I swiped them away. "When I heard the music, heard you play, it brought back memories for me. Now he's gone and I..."

Gavin wrapped his arms around me, drawing me into his embrace. His licorice scent filtered into my senses, warm and soothing. Firm beneath my cheek, the broad planes of his chest rose and fell as he breathed.

I hadn't intended to tell him about my father, share my memory with him. In my effort to console Gavin, he'd ended up comforting me.

Gavin traced his fingers through my hair, petting me, easing me. The contradiction between his gruff exterior and his tender ministrations wasn't lost on me.

"I'm sorry for your loss. You must've loved your father very much." Gavin's voice, smooth as silk, wormed its way deep inside my chest, working its magic. I leaned into him, soaking up his comfort like a flower eager for water.

"Yes, I did." I smiled. "You know, I did something today, something he would've been proud of."

"What's that?" Gavin continued to stroke my hair, trailing his fingers along my bare arm in the process. His gentle, tender touch lit my skin with fire at each brush.

"I auditioned at the Oregon Ballet Theater."

He stiffened, the muscles beneath my fingers hardening like steel before he relaxed. His strength lit a fire deep inside, and I sucked my bottom lip between my teeth, nibbling on the edge.

As if he could sense my reaction, a soft masculine groan of frustration eased from him. "When will you find out?"

"Not for a couple of weeks." For some reason, I couldn't bring myself to tell him that even if I received an offer, I'd have to turn it down. Maybe I just wasn't ready to share my secret with him.

Gavin drew me away to stare into my eyes. With a longing in his gaze that surprised me, he skimmed his finger over my forehead, placing a stray strand of hair behind my ear. "You look very lovely tonight."

At least he hadn't used the dreaded word. I smiled.

A tic pulsed to life under his eye. "Did you follow my instructions?"

"Panties are an unnecessary distraction." Heat flared from my chest, up my neck, and into my cheeks.

He chuckled. "I'll take that as a 'yes.' How I love to make you blush. The rush of blood through your veins is so alluring."

Slipping his hand down my bare arm, my skin tingled, electrified from his touch. Gavin grasped my fingers and drew me toward the lone chair by the fireplace. Similar to last time, a warm fire crackled in the hearth.

"What do you want me—" Before I finished my sentence, he set his finger against my lips. Warm and calloused from his instrument, the roughness prickled my skin.

"Shh." A smile tugged at his mouth, pulling the skin taut around the mask. "No questions."

I swallowed, anticipation strumming along my nerves. His gaze riveted on my throat before returning to my eyes. He slid off his jacket and hung it on one of the coat rack's pegs.

His muscles bulged under his shirt, his biceps flexing as he undid the first two buttons. Smooth and silky, his skin glowed from the firelight, and the urge to touch his chest, feel the taut muscles made my hand jerk.

His brow furrowed. "Don't worry, Alexandra. This time will be much more pleasurable, I promise."

With the glint in his eye, I had no doubt, but I was in over my head. My experiences with Allen had in no way prepared me to be a courtesan. Why had I thought I could do this? To save my life, that's why. Gavin had promised a double payment, and that was something I couldn't turn down.

"Okay, what…"

Deliberate and slow, he wrapped one arm around my waist and drew me to him. My palms landed on his shirt, his muscles tensing beneath my fingertips.

A short squeal burst from my lips, and my heartbeat picked up its pace.

Gavin slid his hand down my back while he captured my chin with the thumb and forefinger of his free hand.

"No questions, remember?" The deep timbre of his voice rumbled from his chest into mine.

My nipples hardened in response, pressing into him.

"Ah, yes, that's much better. Your excitement feeds my own." The fire's soft glow reflected along the mask, lighting up the intricate scrollwork. He ran his thumb over my bottom lip, pulling at the tender flesh.

Out of reflex more than anything, my tongue darted between my lips, moistening them and circling his thumb in the process. Warm and enticing, the flavors of licorice and spices filled my senses. Gavin brought his lips to mine, brushing them with a barely-there kiss.

Blissful tingles tickled my lips, and I groaned, eager for more. He deepened the kiss and slid his tongue along the sensitive nerves, requesting entrance. I obliged, opening for him, and he took advantage, exploring me with a fevered intensity I'd never experienced before. When at last he broke the kiss, our panting breaths echoed in the space between us.

"Alexandra, you tease me." He trailed delicate kisses from my lips, over my chin, and down my neck. As he tugged me closer, his arousal pressed against my hip. I inhaled at the length and breadth of him. Oh my...oh my, indeed.

As a courtesan, it was my job to please him. I took a deep breath, slid my hand in the small gap between us, and wrapped my fingers around his long, firm erection.

A groan of pure masculine need escaped his lips.

I smiled, feminine pride filling my chest. Why the other courtesans feared him, I didn't have a clue. A little brusque on the surface, he seemed gentle and caring on the inside. Taking a step back, I trailed my fingers up each button of his shirt until I came to the top one. The first two, already undone, didn't need my attention, so I gripped the next in line and slid the button through the eye hole.

Gavin grabbed my wrist. "The shirt stays on."

I peered at him, searching what I could see of his features not hidden behind the mask. Determination lined his brow, but his eye held a wariness I hadn't seen before.

Had I done something wrong? I wanted to ask, but the words wouldn't come. The crackle of the fire and our heated breaths were the only sounds in the room. At last, my voice returned. "All right."

He relaxed, releasing my hands and kissing me at the corner of my lips. "It's not you, Alexandra, believe me, it's not you."

Encouraged by his words and a boldness that surprised me, I

tugged at his belt buckle. The stiff leather didn't want to cooperate, and he wrapped his fingers around mine, easing the belt from the loop with ease. With a flick of my finger, the zipper slipped down its track.

I couldn't help it, I had to look. My breath caught in my throat. The tip of his erection poked over the edge of his underwear. I rubbed a fingertip over the soft crown.

He jerked and gripped my shoulders. A hiss eased from his lips. "By the dark gods, you drive me insane."

My chest expanded at his impassioned reaction. Emboldened, I pulled at his pants.

He toed off his boots and helped me rid him of his trousers.

Long, firm, and proud, his erection jutted straight out from his abdomen. I slipped to my knees and wrapped my fingers around the velvety skin that covered his hard shaft. As I stroked my palm over the sensitive flesh, the end glistened with his arousal.

A shudder rippled down his legs, and he buried his fingers in my hair, grasping at the strands. "You toy with me."

"Do I?" Shocked at my boldness, I smiled and swirled my tongue over his tip, lapping up the small bead. The salty taste had a hint of his natural dark licorice.

While I stroked him, I eased my mouth over his crown, sliding my teeth along the exquisite edge. His grip in my hair tightened, but he was careful not to hurt me.

Working him back and forth, I cupped his heavy sac with my free hand. We moved in a rhythm, matched only by his heated breaths and my moans.

"That's enough." Gavin pulled away, wrapped his fingers around my arms, and drew me upward to stand before him.

My mind swam. "Why did you stop?"

"Women always come first. I prefer it that way." His gaze flicked down my outfit, an adorable, sly smile curling his lip.

"The dress doesn't do you justice, Alexandra. It pales in comparison to your natural, beautiful elegance."

I tried not to flinch at the word, but I couldn't help it, the response a deep-rooted reaction.

He placed his forefinger under my chin, forcing me to look at him. His furrowed brow indicated his concern. "You despise that word. It is my job to make sure you overcome your distaste for it."

His smile returned, and he kissed me, a soft caress that bloomed, becoming more intense, passionate. I melted under his onslaught, aware that he could be more dangerous to me than I'd ever anticipated. The thought scared me more than I cared to admit. I couldn't think about it, not now, so I forced the idea from my mind and enjoyed the kiss.

He slid his hand around to my lower back and, with a possessive tug, drew me closer. Using his free hand, he cupped my breast in his palm and flicked his thumb over my nipple. A zing of excitement travelled along my nerves. My clit pulsed to life.

A slow chuckle eased from his throat. "You respond to me so well, Alexandra. It's as if you were made for me."

Wetness formed at the juncture between my legs, and a shiver of pure need tracked down my spine. What this man could do to me, given the chance. "I…I…" I had no words.

Gavin brushed his fingertip along the edge of the dress, skimming my cleavage then slipping under the garment to graze my nipple once again. Another rush of blood spiraled through me. How I wanted him.

As if he read my mind, he pressed his erection against my thigh, sliding it dangerously close to the juncture between my legs.

I cried out, tightening my grip on his shoulders.

He leaned in and kissed me on the neck, just under my ear. Before I could respond, he slid his arm under my legs, picking me up. My palms landed on his shirt, his pecs rock hard beneath my fingers.

His focused attention traveled to my breasts before returning to my eyes. "I'll come back to those later."

"You promise?" I whispered.

Red flashed in his eye then he smiled. "I promise."

Gavin nestled me in the large wingback chair and kneeled before me. With an exquisite intensity, his gaze never leaving mine, he lifted first one leg then the other and placed them over the chair's arms, spreading me wide. My dress slid up my thighs, baring my most intimate parts to him.

Exposed and vulnerable, a sudden shyness spread over me. My cheeks heated.

A deep rumble, almost a purr, reverberated in Gavin's chest. "Beautiful Alexandra, you glisten with desire, for me."

His eye gleamed with a passion I couldn't ignore. My heart melted, just a bit, but I couldn't allow that. He was a vampire. I was a courtesan. Our relationship was strictly business.

He gripped my thighs, spreading my legs a touch further. The white skin of my mound, freshly shaved, peeked from under my dress. He pressed his lips against the inside of my thigh, moving ever closer. I trembled with each contact, but just when he was close enough to kiss the juncture between my legs, he retreated.

I moaned my protest and raised my hands, grasping the back of the chair.

"I have to be even." Gavin smiled and turned to my other leg. As he kissed his way up my thigh, the edge of his mask brushed against my bare skin. The cool metal was a welcome relief against my hot, achy flesh. When he reached my mound, he slid his tongue over my lips with long, languorous strokes.

My hips bucked and my nails dug into the chair's back. A new experience for me, the electrifying sensations were almost more than I could handle.

His hold on my thighs tightened, and he swirled his tongue

over my folds, circling me with his talented caresses. With each revolution, he paid extra attention to my clit, tormenting me. My breathing increased in tempo with his ministrations. On the next pass, I lost control, and the wave overtook me, spiraling through me in sheer delight.

Gavin held on, pulling every last shudder from me. At last, he let me go. Licking his lips, he smiled. "That will do. For a starter."

"Starter?" I croaked.

"Oh, yes." Gavin moved closer, trailing kisses along the dress over my stomach until he reached my breasts. "I've ignored these for far too long."

A small giggle escaped my lips. "Really?"

"Really." He tugged on my sleeve. "Let's get you out of this confining garment."

As the material fell away from my shoulder, his attention riveted on my arm. He blinked, and the lines around his eyes tightened as a look of sheer horror passed over his features. Faster than I thought possible, he stood, backing away, hands fisting at his side. "Those marks. How did you get them?"

I scrambled to stand and yanked up my sleeve. "I bruise easily." At this moment and under these circumstances, there was no way I could tell him I was sick. I'd enjoyed my time with him and didn't want to see it end.

"Get out." Gavin's voice was low, controlled.

Confusion clouded my mind, his turnabout whipping me like wind from a violent storm. "I don't understand. Why are you—"

"I said, 'Get out!' " He picked up his pants and jerked them on, shoving his still hard member out of the way as he zipped up the fly.

I placed my hand along his back. "Gavin—"

He whirled on me. Red burned in his good eye, and his fangs glistened in the firelight. "What part of 'get out' do you not understand?"

My heart stuttered, but I wouldn't give up on him, not yet. "But what's wrong? What can I do—"

He grabbed the table and flung it across the room where it crashed against the bookcase. Several books fell to the ground. Bits of broken wood shards scattered across the polished wood floor.

I bolted for the door, not bothering to grab my shoes.

The pictures on the hall were a blur as I ran down the corridor. My breath heaved from my lungs.

When I reached the entryway, I flung open the door and raced down the steps.

"Alexandra, wait." Gavin's voice, etched with regret, halted me.

I turned, my bare feet cold against the entryway's paved stones. My beating heart pounded in my ears.

He stood in the doorway. Silhouetted by the hall light, I couldn't see his features. "I'm sorry. Please, don't go."

I shook my head as I backed over the stones. A part of me screamed to stay, to return to him, but the fear coursing through my veins had me in its grasp.

The limo's engine roared to life, and a twinge of relief flickered inside me. Before I could change my mind, I dashed down the pathway. When I reached the car, I glanced over my shoulder.

Gavin stood in the doorway, his forearms pressed against the trim. By the stiffness in his shoulders, anguish radiated from him in waves. He leaned forward as if to take a step, his foot hovering over the welcome mat. A tremor wracked his body. With a firm shove, he pushed away from the entrance. A feral cry erupted from his lips. It was as if he couldn't cross the threshold.

I yanked open the car door and slid into the seat.

"Are you all right?" Max's smooth voice carried in the small space.

I let loose the breath I hadn't realized I'd held. "Yeah. I'm fine. Please, take me home."

The car sped down the driveway, and I leaned my head against the window. After tonight's episode, I'd never see Gavin again. Perhaps that was for the best.

Because I'd met the vampire the other courtesans feared.

~

GAVIN

Heat from the fire blasted over my face, and the silver in my mask burned hot against my skin. Mesmerized by the flames licking the firewood, my mind replayed the disastrous scene with Alexandra. The bruises on her arm, round and dark, had looked like fingerprints. My fingerprints. A bead of sweat dribbled along the mask's edge, irritating the bare skin at my cheek. I swiped the moisture away.

Frustration bubbled along my nerves. Every time I approached the front door, the shakes and a river of sweat burst over my skin, keeping me inside. Maybe it was a good thing I'd trapped myself in this home. Otherwise, I would've gone after Alexandra.

I turned from the fire and paced the large open space, my expensive Ferragamos slapping against the floor. A danger to all women, I'd proved yet again why I needed to remain inside. I was a monster who frightened them into running from me.

My gaze drew to the wingback chair. Memories of Alexandra's legs spread over the arms, her wet, glistening cleft, open and inviting, flicked across my mind. I'd wanted nothing more than to please her. Subsisting on bottled blood helped stave off the need to feed, but I couldn't deny how much I wanted to sink my teeth into the graceful little courtesan.

I pinched the bridge of my nose and exhaled, long and slow. A distraction, that's what I needed. I strode to the Stradivarius and gripped my favorite instrument. As I strummed the bow over the strings, the music echoed off the walls.

As if in a dream, I saw a ballerina prance across a stage, pirouetting to the sound of my violin. Her fluid movements, graceful and full of passion, captivated me. I hadn't experienced anything like that in decades. Longing tightened my chest, a spark of need and desire so powerful I couldn't breathe. I glanced to her face, but the light cast shadows over her features. Only her blonde hair and beautiful pale skin were discernible, yet I had no doubt of her identity.

I stopped playing, the last chord reverberating around the sparse room. A sudden warmth crept under my skin. This courtesan, Alexandra, had slipped her way past my defenses. Unleashing my temper, I'd scared her. She deserved an apology for my impulsive, barbaric behavior.

I must see her again.

Even as the words solidified in my mind, fear wrapped its fingers around my chest. She'd be better off staying as far away from me as possible. Not only was I dangerous, I was selfish, too. Self-loathing sent bile up my throat, yet I wouldn't relent until she came here again.

CHAPTER 7

LEXI

"*L*exi, please, eat something. The doctor said you need to keep up your strength." Miranda squeezed my shoulder.

I peered at the scrambled eggs and bacon getting cold on my plate. The scent of bacon in the morning used to be pleasant, but today, it sickened me and churned my stomach.

I pushed the plate away. "I'm sorry, I can't." Both my illness and my concern over how I'd left things with Gavin caused my lack of appetite. Even though it had been several days since I'd seen him, I couldn't forget about our last encounter.

Miranda crossed her arms and furrowed her brow, but underneath the tough bravado, worry lines rimmed her eyes. "Don't tell me you're still thinking about that asshat vampire, Gavin."

I exhaled. "You know me so well, don't you?"

A smile bloomed on her face. "Better than anyone. You need to forget about him."

I directed my gaze through the window at the golden leaves

on the tree, or rather, what was left of them. "But he paid me, even though I didn't do anything for him."

Heat rose to my cheeks. Once again, he'd pleased me, but he hadn't taken any of my blood. After his violent outburst, I'd bolted like a scared cat, thankful I'd made it out of his place before he'd caught me. Who knows what he would've done?

He'd called me three times since then, but I'd let voicemail pick up the calls. There were no messages. I wasn't sure what to think.

Miranda scooped up my plate and tossed my breakfast remains down the garbage disposal. The whir of the machine as the water slipped down the hole echoed throughout the room. When it stopped, she peered at me over her shoulder. "You ready to go to your appointment?"

"You bet." I scooted the chair away from the table and stood. A sharp pain ricocheted from my spine, down my arm, and into my hand. Numbness tingled my fingers. White spots formed in my vision. I gripped the back of the chair to steady myself.

Miranda was there in an instant. She wrapped her arms around my shoulder. "Hey, you all right? You went pale for a moment."

My vision cleared, and I forced a laugh to set Miranda at ease. "My hand fell asleep, that's all."

Miranda tugged me against her, and her warm scent, like fresh apples, filtered into my senses. "I'm worried about you, Lexi, worried a lot."

I pulled away and met my best friend's gaze. My throat tightened, my eyes brimming with tears. "Everything'll be all right. No need to worry."

The furrow in her brow returned. "You're holding something back. Please, tell me."

I exhaled. "Fine, you'll find out at some point anyway. At my last appointment, the doctor told me the cancer was on a fast track. He hasn't given the treatment good odds."

Miranda clasped my fingers. "No, no, no, no. You have to fight this."

"I will, I'm not giving up on my dream to dance, and—"

The beep, beep, beep of my phone cut off my words. I tugged the device from my jeans pocket and glanced at the caller ID. Unlisted. A flash of anger descended over me like a cloud. With every intention of telling Gavin off, I slid my finger across the screen.

"Alexandra." Gavin's smooth voice, sexy as hell, slipped over the airwaves.

My pulse picked up another notch. "Gavin, what do you want?"

"Don't talk to that bastard. End the call, Lexi." Miranda gripped my hand, but I yanked away and stepped toward the kitchen window.

Gavin exhaled. "Your friend is right. I'm not very nice at times. My sincerest apologies for my behavior the other night. I was out of line."

His deep, soothing baritone worked its way inside, warming me to him. "I don't understand why you were so angry."

Miranda tugged on my arm. "Lexi, we should go."

I covered the phone's microphone with my finger. "Go start the car, I'll be right down."

She narrowed her gaze, evaluating me. After a long moment, she huffed. "Okay, but if you're not there in ten minutes, I'm coming back to drag your ass down there."

Love for Miranda wrapped around me like a familiar blanket. I was lucky to have her. "Absolutely, and if I'm late, I'll even let you beat me with a wet noodle. Okay?"

"I'll hold you to that." She smiled, grabbed her purse, and slipped out the door.

I returned my attention to the vampire on the other end of the line. "Gavin, I don't understand what happened, why you reacted so...strongly. Did I do something wrong or offend you in some way?"

"It wasn't you. I'm to blame. Tell me, was I too rough with you? Did I hurt you?"

I rubbed my forehead. "Hurt me? No, of course not." On the contrary, he'd given me more pleasure than I'd ever experienced before. Memories of his kisses tingled my thighs, the sensation tracing his path. I stifled a groan.

A low sigh of relief slid over the connection. "That's good. For a moment there, I thought I'd... But then how did you get those bruises on your arm?"

Understanding dawned. "You didn't hurt me. My bruises, they're not from you."

A low growl reverberated through the phone. "Then who? Tell me."

His protectiveness sent a thrill tingling along my nerves. "No one. I just bruise easily." *Especially now that I'm sick.*

"If anyone had touched you..." Though incomplete, his threat was clear.

Curiosity got the better of me, and I blurted the question burning at the back of my mind. "Why did you call?"

Gavin exhaled a long breath. "I couldn't stop thinking about you and how badly I'd behaved. I wanted to offer my sincerest apology, but more than that, I want to see you again."

"I'm not sure that's a good idea." I wasn't sure I could handle another angry outburst.

"You mentioned you loved to dance. Please dance for me. I'll pay you a nice bonus and promise to be on my best behavior."

"Your best behavior." Doubt tinged my words. "How do I know you won't get pissed off again?"

"If it would make you feel better, Max can remain in the house." Gavin's conciliatory tone was unmistakable. "Although I'd prefer a private dance."

"Why?" A part of me wanted to give in to his demands, but another, more cautious side, held me back.

"I don't leave my home, and I miss live theater, dance in particular. It's been a very long time since I've seen anyone perform. I especially love ballet. The sounds of the orchestra, the energy of the dancers as they twirl, pirouette, and prance across the stage fills me with a passion..."

His love for live theater reverberated in his tone. My mutual admiration for everything ballet, with the dancers, the stage-hands, the lighting crew, and the musicians in the orchestra pit, swelled deep inside me. For several minutes, our conversation ventured into a discussion about the ballets we'd seen, our favorites, and which dancers inspired us. At long last, Gavin returned to his original request. "Alexandra, will you dance for me?"

My gaze tracked to the window. A leaf, golden-kissed by the sun, slipped from the tree's branch and floated away.

"Life is fleeting, follow your heart." My father's words bubbled to the surface of my mind. Allen, that asshat, had belittled my love of dance, saying it was a stupid, impossible dream. Gavin, on the other hand, seemed genuinely interested.

I shouldn't do this, shouldn't see this temperamental vampire, but I couldn't seem to resist. I took a large breath. "As long as Max is in the house, I'd love to perform for you, but please, no money. You paid me when I hadn't even completed my courtesan duties—"

"I'm so glad to hear that you'll return. Max will pick you up at sunset. Beautiful Alexandra, I look forward to watching you perform." The click of the line echoed in my ear.

What had I done? Was I crazy? He'd terrified me the last time we'd met. Yet, something about the reclusive, moody vampire called to me, and despite my fears, my chest fluttered with antic-ipation.

CHAPTER 8

LEXI

"*L*exi, we're here." Max's deep voice woke me up.

My fingers tightened around something smooth and hard, confusion toying with me. As the scent of the limo's leather interior filtered into my senses, the tension in my shoulders eased, and I released my grip on the armrest.

"Thanks, Max. You win the award as the best driver in town. I didn't feel a single bump." I rubbed my finger under my eye, careful not to smear my mascara.

He glanced at me in his rearview mirror. Even in the dim light, I could see a wry smile tugging at his lip. "My pleasure. You fell asleep pretty fast. Must've had a long day."

I smiled. My tiredness had nothing to do with a busy day. The radiation knocked me for a loop. My back had ached something fierce, and I'd resorted to some pain meds which put me to sleep for most of the afternoon. Although the pain had subsided, the grogginess took a while to wear off. Guess I'd needed a few more winks.

My eyes rimmed with hot tears. Even with the treatments, my chance of survival didn't look good. Angry at myself for letting my emotions get the better of me, I pursed my lips and blinked the wetness away. Tumor or not, I refused to give up on my dream to dance on the live stage, even if it was only once.

Max slid from his seat and shut the door with a soft click. A few seconds later, the door on my right opened and a waft of cool night air slid along my bare arms. Dressed in a leotard and pair of tights, I hadn't bothered to cover the bruises or red splotches. Gavin had already seen them, so what was the point?

Max held out his hand, and I took it. We'd been through this routine before, so I knew the drill. When Max picked me up, he'd dropped off the shoes I'd left behind from my last visit. This time, though, I carried my ballet shoes and a bag with some extra clothes.

"May I help you with those?" Max nodded to my small duffle.

"Thanks, but I've got it." I peered at the house. A light brightened the library window, shadowing the figure of a large man—Gavin. A zing of excitement mixed with trepidation slid along my nerves.

Max cleared his throat. "I'll be in the kitchen tonight. Ester, Gavin's housekeeper, made a special dinner for you, at his request."

I met the limo driver's gaze. "Gavin's outbursts are downright scary. Why is he so angry?"

Max placed his hand on my elbow and guided me up the stone steps. He adjusted his collar, a sadness tightening his handsome features. "That, my dear, is something I'm not at liberty to say, but if you want to know, ask him yourself. What I can tell you is he's more bark than bite. Well," he chuckled, "you know what I mean."

Curiosity drew my attention to the window once again, but the shadowed figure was gone.

At the top of the stairs, Max gripped the door handle and

pushed on the latch. The massive wooden door swung open, its hinges issuing a soft creak.

"After you," Max ushered me inside. One of his fangs protruded over his bottom lip, glowing from the entryway's bright light.

I stepped over the threshold. A tingle raced down my spine. I had the sense that tonight would be different, and Danae, the tarot card reader's words slipped through my mind. *"Fear of change is inevitable. Resistance is useless."*

As Max closed the door, the hinges squeaked again, echoing down the long hall. He gave me a quick nod. "You know the way. I'll be in the kitchen. Come find me when you're ready to leave."

I swallowed and tightened my grip on my bag. "Thanks, Max."

He hurried past me, and I watched until he disappeared through a doorway, his large frame squeezing by. Well, now I knew which room was the kitchen.

My attention tracked to the library door. I strained, listening for the slightest sounds, but all I heard was the rhythmic tick, tick, tick of the large grandfather clock halfway down the hall. Gathering up my courage, I approached the door and rapped my fingers against the wood.

"Enter." Even through the solid grain, Gavin's voice wrapped around me, pulling me forward like a strong breeze.

I grasped the handle and pushed open the door.

The scent of roast beef, mashed potatoes, and fresh baked bread washed over me. My stomach rumbled. Food and I weren't on the best terms lately, but this smelled wonderful. A covered platter sat on a small table, which had been added next to the wingback chair.

A fire blazed in the fireplace. Wood popped and crackled, sending out sparks. I glanced from the curtains to the long row of books lining the wall to where Gavin leaned against the bar.

My heart stuttered. I drew in a quick breath.

Gavin rested his arms along the bar, his broad shoulders

hunched forward. He wore a elegant tailored suit and a pair of dress shoes. White cuffs extended from beneath the suit's sleeves, in sharp contrast to the dark material. He turned his attention to me, twirling a glass of wine, the liquid blood red and rich, his silver mask reflecting the chandelier's light. "Welcome, Alexandra. It's good to see you again."

"G…Gavin." My cheeks heated from tripping over his name.

"You blush for me already. How endearing." He straightened, and his shoulders tugged the material tight around his biceps, accentuating his firm muscles.

My fingers twitched with the urge to run my hands over the elegant material and feel the steel beneath. I bit my lip, and drew my attention from his shirt to his gaze.

His lip curled into a grin. "You are happy to see me as well. That is good, very good indeed. May I offer my sincerest apology for my reaction the other night? It won't happen again."

"You promise?" The words slipped from my mouth before I could stop them.

He raised his eyebrow over his one good eye. "If that is what you need from me. Then, yes, I promise. Here," he raised the glass of red wine, "I poured this for you. Come, share a drink from my collection."

I took a step forward, then another, as if my body had a mind of its own. Setting my shoes and my bag on the bar, I slid my fingers around the smooth glass stem. He didn't release his hold, but instead, trailed the pad of his thumb along the back of my middle finger. His rough, calloused skin teased my sensitive flesh.

A shiver of desire raced up my arm, and a tendril of excitement wound its way to my core. I held my breath.

His gaze shifted from my face, traveling over my shoulders and down my body. All the while, his thumb continued to stroke my finger. "You came prepared to dance. That pleases me."

"Yes, I did." With his soft caress working its magic on me, I might do anything he asked.

As his attention returned to my eyes, a spark of red flashed in his iris. His smile returned, and an adorable dimple formed in his good cheek. "My housekeeper, Ester, made you a lovely dinner. Would you like to eat before or after you perform?"

I swallowed, the stroke of his thumb more distracting than I'd ever imagined. "It's best if I perform on an empty stomach."

He nodded, and a lock of his dark hair dislodged itself from behind his ear. The strands graced his cheek, and I had to resist the urge to push them back into place. With a calculated smile, he released my hand. The glass shook in my grasp, the wine coming dangerously close to the lip. I took a small sip then set it down on the bar.

He clasped my fingers in his grasp and brought my hand to his lips. With an intensity burning in his gaze, he kissed the back of my finger, the same one he'd stroked with such care. My insides quivered with need, and wetness moistened the juncture between my legs. Embarrassment flared in my cheeks, warming them.

"Alexandra, your shyness is so endearing. I must remember I promised you I'd behave. Dance for me now before I change my mind and want something else instead." A wicked smile bloomed over his face, and he released my hand.

My heart stuttered. I missed his touch already. "Let me put on my ballet shoes."

He nodded, strode across the room, removed his coat, and hung it on the rack. Under his white shirt, his muscles flexed beneath the thin material. Mesmerized, I couldn't look away. Tenderly, he lifted his Stradivarius from its case, grabbed his bow, and nestled the instrument beneath his chin. A moment later, the soft strains of a musical scale filled the room, in the key of "G" if I wasn't mistaken.

I sat on the floor, and the edge of my short skirt lay across my tights at mid-thigh. For tonight's dance, I'd selected my pink outfit. Gavin had said pink was his favorite color on me.

I leaned forward, and a twinge ran from my back down my right arm. Warmth burned at the site, reminding me of my earlier treatment. I gritted my teeth and vowed my disease wouldn't get in the way. Not tonight.

While I laced up my left shoe, a string from the frayed ends unraveled from the material. I yanked on the elusive strand, but it wouldn't come free. Instead, I tucked the rough ends under the knot. As I tugged on my right shoe, I stole a glance at Gavin.

He closed his eye and cradled the violin against his cheek. With a grace and beauty that defied his Jekyll and Hyde disposition, his fingers slid over the strings, caressing them with devoted reverence. Despite my better judgment, I wanted him to play me like that, give me the same kind of special love and attention.

I bit the inside of my lip as my chest heaved. It was better for both of us if I kept this on a business level. Besides, there was no guarantee I'd survive my cancer. Tonight, I just wanted to dance and enjoy his company.

I rose to my feet. I used the edge of the bar to stretch, placing my heel on the polished wood and warming the muscles in my leg. As I continued my warm-up routine, I snagged glimpses of Gavin. He moved on from the scales, the tones of a light melody filling the room. The song wasn't one I recognized, but the soft, pleasant notes eased under my skin, relaxing me. When I finished my stretches, I padded to the middle of the room.

Gavin stopped mid-strain and glanced at me. A smile lit up his features, and one of his fangs protruded over his plump bottom lip. "You're ready."

I nodded and placed the heel of my left foot next to the instep on my right in the classic ballerina turn-out pose.

"What shall I play for you?" The smooth timbre of his voice drifted across the space between us.

I relaxed my arms at my sides, hands cupped inward. "*Swan Lake* opus 20, number 13 *Danse Des Cygnes*, if you don't mind."

His eye sparked. "As you wish."

He stroked the bow over the strings and the wonderful melody echoed off the wall, caught up in the acoustics in the room. Light from the chandelier lit up the wooden floor like a stage. I began to dance, letting the music seep into my body and my soul.

~

GAVIN

Alexandra grew more beautiful and more dangerous every time I saw her. If I wasn't careful, she'd destroy me in a heartbeat, that is, if I didn't kill her first. My gaze tracked her as she spun and twirled to the sound of the music coming from the Stradivarius. Grace and beauty radiated in her every move from her fingertips to her toes. Mesmerized, I couldn't drag my attention away.

Deep inside, a crack formed around the hard, crusty exterior protecting my heart. Tendrils of hope, desire, and need filtered through the gaps, searching for a way in. I hadn't felt this alive in decades. My breath grew shallow as fear fought to close the hole Alexandra, my beautiful little dancer, had created.

Focusing on her, I poured my love of music into my instrument, showing her what she'd brought to me. Even though we stood several feet apart, it seemed as if she was in my arms, and we were dancing together.

A bead of sweat trickled down my brow and under my collar. How I longed to remove the confining material, but that could never happen. She could never see the hideous scars hidden not only under the mask, but the shirt as well.

Alexandra pirouetted across the room, matching the music's cadence beat for beat. With a grace and beauty I could only admire, she danced as if she'd been born with ballet slippers on her feet. Each arabesque, each plié, each pirouette were full of such passion and heart, I couldn't keep my gaze from her.

The longer she danced, the more mesmerized I became, and my fingers flew over the Stradivarius, my bow becoming an extension of my hand. How I longed to touch her, caress her, make her sing like the strings on my familiar and beloved instrument. My music and her dance melded together until I couldn't differentiate the two. I wanted to close my eyes, give in to the violin's melody, but I wouldn't miss out, not on beautiful Alexandra. I couldn't recall the last time I'd experienced such happiness.

Alexandra continued to dance, and I committed every exquisite move to memory. On a fast strain in the music, she leapt into the air and performed a *grand jeté*. The lace on her left foot unraveled from her ankle. As she landed, the long string caught under her slipper. A cry burst from her lips, and she tumbled to the ground, the skin on her arm sliding along the floor with a loud squeak.

Adrenaline spiked in my veins. I tossed my violin toward its case, not caring if the instrument landed safely or not. Scooping her into my arms, I cradled Alexandra against my chest. My pulse raced, faster than it had in a very long time. "Are you injured?"

Her hands landed on my chest, and she gripped my shirt, bunching the material between her fingers. "No, no. The strap on my ballet shoe broke. It just surprised me, that's all. I should've bought some new ones."

"Thank God you're all right." Not ready to let her go, I carried her to my comfortable wingback chair and sat down. Still planted on my lap, she gripped my arms to steady herself. The skin under my shirt burned, as if an electrical charge filled with desire sparked from her fingertips.

I slid my hand along her thigh, the tights a barrier between us. At her ankle, the frayed ends of a lace stuck out. I fumbled with the strings, loosening them for her. With a quick tug, I removed the shoe and dropped it on the floor. It landed with a soft plop next to the chair.

Beneath the end of her tights, her bare ankle, swollen and red, belied her comments. I peered at her. "Seems you twisted your ankle."

She pushed against my pecs and struggled to stand. "I'm sure it's just a small sprain."

I let her go, and she slid from my seat, her bottom rubbing against my growing arousal.

A grimace crossed her gorgeous features. "Ugh, this is so not what I needed."

I admired her fight, her willingness to not give in to the pain, but I hated seeing her hurt. As I stood, I gently gripped her elbow to support her if she needed me. "What can I do?"

Determination lines etched around her eyes made her seem tired in a way I hadn't noticed before. They didn't detract from her beauty. On the contrary, they spoke of a resolve I had to respect. Her will, her passion, was something I'd lost long ago.

A forced smile tugged at her lip. "Some ice in a bag or a towel would be nice to help with the swelling. Do you have some in the kitchen?"

I swept my arm under her legs and cradled her against my chest. She gripped my shirt once again. A button flew into the air, landed on the floor, and skittered across the polished wood. "What are you doing?"

"Taking you to my room so I can attend to your ankle. There are chemical ice packs in my private bathroom." The hair at my nape rose. I couldn't remember the last time I'd had a woman in my personal quarters. The cast-iron fortification I'd placed around my heart seemed paper thin when I was around her. Still, I couldn't afford to let Alexandra in, for her sake, as well as my own.

CHAPTER 9

LEXI

*G*avin carried me up a grand staircase, one with dark hand-carved railings and a plush carpet that absorbed his footsteps. I tightened my grip on his shirt, the firm planes of his pecs hard against my knuckles. Nestled against him, his warm scent filtered into my senses. I could get used to this.

My ankle wasn't twisted as badly as Gavin thought. I'd rolled it, and the initial shock had made me cry out, but even now, the soreness waned. He wanted to tend to me, and with a look of sincerity in his eye, well, I couldn't refuse him.

As he carried me down a long hallway, I studied his features. The mask covered half his face, from his forehead, over his left eye, and around his cheek. Curiosity tingled my fingers, and I trailed my fingertip along the edge.

Gavin gasped and jerked his head out of the way. "What are you doing?"

"The mask is gorgeous. I wanted to touch the etchings. Did I do something wrong?"

He didn't respond, but the tic under his eye pulsed.

We reached a doorway. He crossed the sill into a large bedroom with a king-size bed nestled against the far wall. Elegant, carved posts cradled the corners of a lovely dark green comforter. The material shimmered in the light emitting from a stained glass lamp resting on a nearby table.

Gavin laid me on the bed, and I sank into the soft duvet.

His gaze flicked over my features. Worry lines formed between his brows. "Stay here. I'll be right back."

Faster than I could track, he dashed through an adjoining doorway. Clinks and pings of metal against porcelain echoed from the washroom. I glanced around. A single claw-foot chair rested against the wall next to the door. Alongside it was a long dresser with a large oval mirror. Polished to a glossy sheen, the wooden top was bare except for a lone picture of a woman. Black and white, the faded photo bore signs of age, but even still, her beauty lit up her features.

A soreness coated the back of my throat. Who was she to Gavin? I didn't have time to dwell on my thoughts as he burst from the room. He held up his fist, eye gleaming with pride, a chemical ice pack clutched in his hand.

"I found it. This will help immobilize your ankle—"

"Gavin."

"So it can heal—"

"Gavin! My ankle will be fine. I rolled it, that's all. See." I slid from the bed, placing a bit of weight on my leg. The ligaments protested, but the pain was manageable. I'd had far worse sprains than this. Although I'd initially thought I'd needed one, an ice pack wasn't necessary.

He closed the distance between us, knelt before me, and ran his fingers over my ankle. A thrilling shiver raced up my leg.

After a quick intake of breath, Gavin's shoulders stiffened. "Did I hurt you?"

My chest constricted. "No, not at all." I trailed my fingers through his dark, silky hair, and his gaze rose to meet mine.

"Alexandra," he licked his lips and swallowed, his Adam's apple undulating in his throat. "That is my biggest fear, that I might..."

He rose and turned his back on me. A shudder wracked his shoulders. "You should leave while you still have time."

Tears pricked my eyes. I ran my fingers along his sleeve until I reached his hand. Sliding my fingers along his, I tugged at him, urging him to face me. "I want to be here, with you."

He flinched, but turned to look at me. Though sadness lined his features, hope gleamed in his eye. "Why?"

I swallowed past the lump in my throat. "No one has taken an interest in me, in my dancing, not since my father. With you, I feel special. I want to know more about you," I placed my palm over his chest right above his heart, "about the man inside."

His gaze narrowed. "You won't like what you find. That, I guarantee."

"Why don't you let me decide?"

A chagrinned smile curled his lip, revealing one of his pointed fangs. "Very well, but don't say I didn't warn you. Ask away."

I swallowed the lump in my throat. "Who's the lady in the picture?"

His attention focused on the old photograph. Tension lines formed around his eye. "That's no lady."

Before I could respond, he darted to the bureau, his shoulders stiff. With more force than necessary, he slammed the picture facedown on the dresser top. Good thing the frame didn't have any glass or it would've shattered.

I placed my hands on my hips. "She must've been important or you wouldn't have a picture of her on your dresser."

He chuckled, but there was no mirth in his tone. "She's the reason for this," he pointed to his mask, "and why I'm here today, as a vampire."

I strode over to him, trailed my finger over the etched silver, then looked into his eye. "Tell me what happened."

His eye tracked back and forth as he studied me.

I held my breath. Would he trust me? Share his past with me?

After a long moment, he exhaled, and the tension in his shoulders visibly eased. "She was attractive, much like you," he brushed his fingers over my forehead and down my short braid, "except her beauty was only skin deep."

My pulse picked up speed. His words beat against my psyche as my brain processed his meaning. Gavin saw beyond my appearance to the person I was inside. My throat tightened, even as a sense of happiness and rightness lightened my spirit.

"I was thirty-two when I met Lorraine in an expensive restaurant in Manhattan. She flaunted herself, teasing me with her charm. My wife had died during childbirth. I still mourned her and my newborn child. I was vulnerable, and Lorraine knew it." He drew away and strode to the bureau. He studied himself in the mirror then peered at me through the tinted glass. "I courted her for three weeks. Should've guessed something wasn't quite right when she wouldn't meet me during the day."

I bit my lip. "She was a vampire?"

He nodded. "One night in 1911, I took her to the Metropolitan Opera House to see a ballet, *Swan Lake*. She seemed so happy, so content. My heart soared, and I thought I'd found someone with whom I could share my life. Unable to contain my elation, I leaned next to her ear and whispered that I loved her." He fisted his hand at his side. Pain and anger radiated from him in waves. "I don't know why I'm telling you this. Not since that night have I shared this information with anyone."

An ache built at the back of my throat. "*Swan Lake*. Is that why you play it, to remember her?"

He snorted. "Lorraine laughed when I confessed my love. I thought it was in shyness. How wrong I'd been. After the performance, she led me to a quiet spot behind the building. Said she wanted some private time to share something with me."

A tingling sensation of fear slid down my spine, leaving goosebumps in its wake. "What did she do?"

"She bit me, almost ripping my throat out in the process." Gavin tugged the edge of his collar away from his throat. Just over his collarbone, two large punctures scarred his skin. "She told me I was one of many. Said she enjoyed the game. To top it off, she scored her wrist and forced me to drink her blood, turning me into a vampire against my will."

I approached him, wanting, no, needing, to touch him, feel his strength and passion. When I was close enough, I rested my hand on his sleeve. "I understand. Becoming a vampire is something I wouldn't want either. Tell me the rest."

He gripped my hand, holding on so tightly, I winced. "I didn't stir until the first rays of the sun rose over the horizon. Burning skin will wake you in an instant."

I gasped. "Your mask."

He nodded. "I lost the eyesight in my left eye and my sense of smell in the process, although I kept the ability to taste bitter and sweet. From that moment forward, I vowed never to do to another what she'd done to me."

Realization dawned on me. "The sun, that's why you won't go outside, isn't it?"

His silence was all the confirmation I needed. I stepped closer, closing the distance between us. He placed his arm around my waist, the movement tender yet sensual. A spark of awareness rippled across my skin. "May I see? I promise not to scream, run, or laugh."

Gavin studied me. I held his gaze, willing him to trust me. At last, he nodded, the brief tilt of his head almost imperceptible.

I brushed my fingers over the silver, admiring the etched detail. "Whoever made your mask did an outstanding job of craftsmanship."

The tension in Gavin's shoulders didn't ease, but he rubbed his hand along my lower back as if he'd appreciated my compliment. I tugged at the string, releasing one end from under his ear. The elastic loosened, and the mask slid into my open palm. I lowered my hand.

Twisted with scarring from his burns, the left side of his face had an odd, pale sheen. His left eye, milky and white stared at me, but it didn't focus. He'd said he was blind. I glanced to his good eye.

His penetrating, evaluating stare bore into me, as if he waited for me to flinch.

I didn't blink or look away. "May I touch you?"

Gavin wiped his hand over his face and his grip along my waist tightened, but he didn't tell me 'no.'

I brushed my fingers along his hairline and over where his brow would've been if he'd had any eyebrow hair. The scar tissue was soft beneath my fingers. "Your skin is so smooth."

He blinked, and his eyelash hairs tickled the back of my fingers. Why the sun had burned away his brow, but not his eyelashes was a wonder. I continued on my path over his cheek and to his chin where the rough patch of stubble grew over his unblemished skin.

"It's an ugly mess. Have you had your fill?" His terse words were in sharp contrast to his gentle caress along my back.

"I think it adds character. You should—"

He yanked the mask from my grip and moved to place it over his scar.

I grasped his wrist, stopping him. "Please, don't. I'd prefer to see you as you really are."

The tic started under his eye once again, but he swallowed several times, his Adam's apple bobbing in a fast rhythm. "As you wish."

He pitched the mask onto the dresser where it landed on top of the overturned picture. An image of Gavin watching a performance of *Swan Lake* with this female vampire made my stomach churn. I peered at him. "Why do you keep her picture, and why do you continue to play *Swan Lake*? Are you some kind of masochist?"

He met my gaze. "I guess the answer to the last question could be 'yes.' The answer to the first two is the same, to never forget."

Anger simmered under my skin, pulsing at my temple. "I don't understand. She changed you, why do you have a shrine for her?"

He blinked. "It's not a shrine. It's a warning, a remembrance of what I've done."

"What you've done?" Confusion clouded my mind.

"Didn't the other courtesans tell you why they fear me so much?"

Dread tugged at my insides, twisting them into a coil. "Your temper. I'm afraid your outbursts are very well known. What the courtesans don't understand is why you won't leave your home."

He tsked, his lip curling at the corner. "You assumed fear of the sun is what keeps me here. The truth is far darker. I remain hidden in my home to keep the monster that I am locked up inside."

"Monster?" I'd seen his anger, but he was far from a monster.

"Lorraine never gave me a choice on whether I wanted to be a vampire. For months I searched, intent on confronting her, but," he ran his hand over his face, "when I found her she was in the process of killing another man. In an uncontrolled fit of rage, I murdered her."

My heart skipped a beat. He'd told me this to scare me, push me away. I clamped my jaw tight and raised my chin. "Do you think you're evil now because of it?"

Gavin took a step back, his hand sliding away from my waist. His mouth opened and closed for a moment before he pursed his lips. "I'm a vampire. Isn't that the embodiment of evil?"

My chest constricted, pain for him tightening around my

lungs until I couldn't breathe. "Did you ever think, that maybe, just maybe, what you did was heroic?"

A stifled laugh erupted from his lips. "Heroic? I murdered her," he held up his palms, "with my bare hands."

The tormented look in his eye beat against my heart, worming its way inside. I cared for him, more than I should. Fighting back tears, I swallowed. "I'll bet you saved a lot of men's lives in the process."

Gavin blinked, his brow furrowing over his deep brown eye. "She wasn't the only one I killed. There was another female there, a newly turned vampire. She seemed scared, innocent, yet in my reckless anger, I murdered her as well."

I took a step toward him, closing the distance between us. "Had she fed on the man, too?"

He exhaled, torment lining his features. "I don't know."

"Perhaps Lorraine trained another to be like her. If you hadn't killed Lorraine and her minion, she would've continued her rampage. You can't blame yourself. What you did was heroic."

His mouth pressed into a grim line. "But what if she was innocent? I didn't give her a chance to explain. I was in a killing rage, and before I knew it, she was dead."

I brushed my fingers along his cheek. "You haven't injured anyone since then, have you?"

He shook his head.

"Stop blaming yourself. You're not the monster you think you are."

"I'm not?"

"You are the most gentle and caring man I know."

Before I could utter another word, he wrapped one arm around my waist and tugged me to him.

I squealed, a flutter tickling my stomach.

Gavin slid his hand along my throat until he cradled my head in his palm. "Alexandra, what you've done to me."

I licked my lips, uncertainty trickling along my veins. "What I've done?"

He drew me closer, bending me backward. His breath tickled my neck. "I had my music, but it wasn't enough. After watching you dance with such passion…" He swallowed. "I've been going through the motions, living, yet not living. You've awoken that in me."

"Gavin…" I buried my hands in his hair and raked my fingernails along his scalp, holding him close. "I'm just a blood courtesan, here to service you."

He pressed soft, silent kisses against my throat, lingering along my carotid artery. "You're more than a courtesan to me."

The back of my throat burned, tightening with his words. "Gavin…I…"

He pulled away enough to look at me. "I want to make love to you, here, in this bed, and I've never brought a woman, courtesan or vampire, to my bed before."

Warm, hot tears coated my eyes. I blinked, trying to keep them at bay, but one slid over my lashes and tracked down my cheek. Gavin caught it with the back of his finger before it could drip from my chin. He studied the small droplet, wet on the edge of his skin. With deliberate intent, he brought his finger to his lips and kissed the tear. "Do you know the old saying?"

"Old saying?"

"If a man kisses a woman's tear, he is bound to her, for forever and a day." The sincerity in his voice stroked me on the inside, warming me.

"I've never heard that one before, but I like it." I couldn't contain my smile as it burst across my face.

He chuckled, and the sound, now familiar and welcome, reverberated from his chest into mine. The sensation tickled my nipples, and they hardened beneath my leotard.

He groaned. "Alexandra, my beautiful little dancer."

For the first time in my life, the dreaded word didn't make me cringe. On the contrary, my chest expanded, filling with a happiness I'd never experienced before. I pressed my breasts against his firm chest.

Gavin swept his hands under my legs and lifted me up, cradling me against him. My laughter echoed off the walls. He yanked away the duvet and set me down on the smooth satin sheets. Cool against the bare skin on my arms, goosebumps rose.

"We can't have that." Gavin's rich baritone voice rumbled with promise.

I raised an eyebrow. "Have what?"

"You cold. I have a special ability to heat up my skin. Allow me to warm you." He knelt on the bed and slid his hands over my one slippered foot and up my tights, his fingers warming me everywhere he touched. "But first, these need to go. Clothes are so restrictive."

CHAPTER 10

GAVIN

$\mathcal{I}$ slid my hands down Alexandra's toned legs, eager to remove her dancer's outfit. In the subdued light from the bedside lamp, her pink leotard reflected against her pale skin, reminding me of how much I adored her rosy cheeks. The need to make her blush sparked my tongue.

"Did you wear pink for me tonight?" I gripped her ankle and tugged on the slipper's laces, untying them with slow, deliberate intent. A gorgeous blush reddened her chest and raced up her throat to her cheeks.

She nibbled her lip. "I remember you liked the color on me."

I chuckled and slid the slipper from her foot. It fell to the carpet with a soft whoosh. Not to ignore the other, injured foot, I stroked my fingers over the slightly swollen ankle. "Is it sore?"

"Not really." She tugged her foot from my grasp and placed it on the bedspread. In the process, her knees parted, and a vision of her wet glistening folds slipped through my mind.

Powerful and quick, the need to have her naked before me

rippled along my nerves. I had to be careful not to hurt her with my strength. "That's good. Very good, indeed."

I placed one knee on the bed and glided my hands up her legs and over her thighs. The leotard was in the way, so I continued my advance, sliding my fingers over her hips and tiny waist.

"That tickles." She squirmed under my touch, her breasts straining against the cloth. Small and round, her nipples peaked in the center.

I couldn't resist. Lowering my head, I coaxed one of the nubs into my mouth. Even through the material, the tip hardened.

"Gavin." She gripped my shoulders, her nails digging into my shirt.

I moaned and scraped my tooth across the fabric, teasing her.

"Gavin, please..."

I peered at her. "My beautiful little dancer, I've only just begun."

A small smile tugged at her lip, part shyness, part anticipation, both endearing.

I raised my eyebrow. "Are you nervous, my sweet?"

"A little." Her blush returned, reddening her cheeks. Then she lifted her chin. "But I want this."

"No worries, my sweet, I'll take good care of you." My erection pressed tight against my pants, pinching my balls. I placed my other knee on the bed, adjusting myself in the process and drew small adoring kisses over her chest and up her throat. When I reached her ear, I nibbled on the tender flesh.

She exhaled, her soft, needful breaths easing deep inside, seeping into my soul. If I wasn't careful with my heart, she'd be the death of me.

"Gavin, these clothes, help me out of them."

I chuckled. "My, my, now who's the impatient one?"

Her eyes gleamed with mirth. "Mine aren't the only clothes that need to come off."

Having no intention of removing my shirt, I ignored her

comment and focused on her outfit, tugging on one strap then the other. Her top slid over her shoulders, baring her breasts for me.

Her peaked nipples stood at attention, ready for my touch. I cupped her breast in my palm, enjoying the weight, and grazed my thumb over the firm tip.

She cried out and wiggled the leotard lower.

My patience with the clothing reached a new low, so I gripped the material bunched at her waist and dragged it over her hips and down her legs, taking the tights with me. With a quick toss, I threw the clothes over my shoulder. They hit the dresser with a smack and slid to the floor.

A giggle emerged from Alexandra's lips. "You look so adorable when you're frustrated."

Her words wound around my chest, tightening like a coil. I struggled to breathe. "Adorable?"

She nodded, her eyes brightening with fondness. "This isn't fair. You should be naked, too."

I nudged her thigh, encouraging her to kneel. As she moved, her breasts bobbed with her exertion. My erection pulsed in response, painful and hard.

She sat on her heels and brushed her hands up my sleeves. "Your muscles are so tight—"

Before she reached the top button on my shirt, I gripped her fingers.

Her gaze rose to meet mine. "What's wrong?"

Lines formed around her eyes, and a rueful heaviness settled onto my shoulders. I hated to see her like that. I brought her fingers to my lips and gave them a gentle kiss. "Nothing, but my shirt stays on."

"What? Why?"

I swallowed. "That's how I prefer it."

She crossed her arms, hiding her breasts from me. "You

removed your mask, yet you won't take off your shirt. Gavin, there's nothing you can't show me."

My fingers twitched with the urge to hide my scarred features. Uncertainty coiled in my stomach, but the look of encouragement on her face fueled my resolve. I clamped my jaw. "All right, but let me do it."

She studied me, then nodded, relaxing onto her heels. I slid my knees off the bed and stood before her. She'd seen the scars on my face, so I shouldn't be nervous. Yet, I was. A bead of perspiration ran down the back of my neck.

I undid each button, sliding the round knob through the eyehole. Alexandra's attention flicked between my eyes and the ever more exposed skin on my chest. When I'd unclasped the last one, I didn't waste any time, but ripped the shirt over my shoulders and let it slip to the carpet.

I held my breath.

Alexandra's gaze roamed over my chest, but it didn't take long before her attention drew to my left arm. I straightened my back, held up my chin, and waited for her reaction.

After a long moment, she exhaled. "This happened that same night, didn't it?"

I nodded and swallowed hard.

"When I look at you, I see strength, courage, and a powerful determination to live. Can I touch it?"

Acceptance, love, and understanding lined her features. My chest hitched, and I released my breath. All I could do was nod.

She inched forward on her knees until she was at the edge of the bed. Placing one hand on my right shoulder for support, she brushed her fingers over my left arm and along the deep pit of my scar. Tenderly, she circled the marred tissue, following the rough, mottled skin over my elbow and to my forearm—or what was left of it.

"This is more damage than from the sun, isn't it? How did this happen?" she whispered.

"My burns were too deep for me to heal."

She planted a kiss on my chin. "I admire your strength. Not everyone would..."

Blood rushed through my veins, drowning out her words. I wrapped my arms around her waist and drew her to me, giving her a bruising kiss. She'd accepted me for who I was, imperfections and all. Completely lost to her now, I would never be the same.

CHAPTER 11

LEXI

*G*avin's kiss sent a tingle of desire all the way to my core. My breasts, sensitive and aroused, pressed against his bare chest, the skin on skin contact lighting up my nerves. I leaned into him, letting him take control, and he slid his hand to the base of my scalp, holding me close.

The bed squeaked from the movement, the sheets soft and silky under my knees. Gavin had bared more than his disfigured skin to me tonight, he'd bared his soul. The scars didn't bother me. They were more a badge of honor than anything else. He'd survived a horrific death and had taken out an evil female predator in the process. Good for him. I couldn't be prouder or love him more. A flush of adrenaline tightened the skin on my scalp. Love him? Did I?

My pulse beat faster. I'd fallen for Gavin, fallen hard and way too fast.

He released me and nuzzled kisses along my neck. "Alexandra, my beautiful little dancer."

His loving words wound their way into my heart and set up home. My fingers brushed over his massive chest, the muscles firm beneath my fingertips. When I reached his abdomen, a line of fine hairs led south. I followed them with eager anticipation.

At the edge of his pants, I gripped his belt and tugged. The shank pulled free of the clasp and his belt hung loose at his waist. I slipped my finger below the seam, my nail skimming the tip of his erection.

He moaned, a feral and deep growl in its most primitive form.

A thrill of excitement spurned me on, and I slid the zipper down, freeing him from his confinement. Long and firm, his erection bobbed from the opening. He toed off his shoes and shoved down his pants, ridding himself of the last bit of clothing.

I cupped his heavy balls in my palm and gripped his shaft, giving him a firm squeeze.

He expelled a quick breath. "You tease me."

The braveness I'd felt the last time I was with him returned full force. "How about I make you come?"

"Beautiful Alexandra, you forget. Ladies first, always." He smiled, the skin pulling tight along his scar.

Before I could respond, he gripped me around the waist and flipped me over. My palms and knees landed on the mattress with a soft whoosh. I squealed in delight.

He climbed on the bed, urging me forward until my hands slid up the headboard and pressed against the wall.

"Much better," he murmured in my ear.

He tossed the pillows onto the floor and snuggled against me. His erection pulsed along my inside thigh, warm and firm. I reached between my legs to grab him, but Gavin gripped my wrist and placed my hand back on the wall.

"Stay here. Let me pleasure you." The command in his voice left no room for argument, but I didn't mind. On the contrary, my legs trembled with anticipation, and a warm wetness moistened the juncture between my legs.

Gavin pressed his chest against my back, tracing soft, poignant kisses along my shoulder. With a tenderness I was fast getting used to, he cupped one breast in his palm and pinched my nipple between his thumb and forefinger. A zip of excitement travelled along my nerves. My breathing increased along with my pulse.

"Very good. I sense your excitement. Are you wet for me?" He knocked his knee against mine, spreading my legs wide. Pressing closer, he placed his erection between my legs, settling himself just under my mound. A needful tremble rippled through me.

While still cupping my breast, he trailed his free hand over my hip, down my stomach, and along the inside of my thigh. Emitting a warm rumble of appreciation, he slipped his finger past my short pubic hairs and between my lips.

A low laugh slipped from him. "Ah, yes, wet indeed. How I wish I could smell your scent."

With smooth strokes, Gavin circled my lips, swirling my own wetness over my clit. Little lightning bolts of excitement flicked along my nerves each time he connected with the sensitive bud. As he continued his ministrations, he placed delicate kisses along my shoulder.

This man had me at his mercy—heart, body, and soul. If only we had more time together. Tears pricked my eyes, and I was glad he couldn't see them.

His rhythm increased, and the smooth skin on his chest rubbed against my back. Sweet kisses of pleasure, he swept his lips along the base of my neck. My skin tingled at the contact. "So lovely."

My breaths eased in and out of my lungs, matching his pace. "Gavin...please."

I couldn't see him smile, but the skin on his chin tightened against my throat. He chuckled. "It would be my pleasure."

The skillful flick of his finger, the tender touches, and the passionate kisses all swirled together in a sudden rush. I couldn't take anymore, exploding in a wash of desire and happiness that took me to the heavens and back.

My vampire held me tight, my back pressed against his chest, and his breath tickled my ear. "My beautiful little dancer, you are more beautiful to me now than ever."

Love for him squeezed my chest with an ache that filled me to the depths of my soul. My emotions raw, I couldn't speak. A soft cry was all that emerged from my throat.

He kissed me along my nape and rubbed his hard erection against my inside thigh. "Are you ready for me?"

"Yes," I whispered. I wanted his hot, hard length inside me, filling me to the brim.

Gavin gripped me around the waist and slid himself along my folds. Slick and warm, my wetness coated him, and the friction threatened another orgasm. I spread my legs wider and leaned forward, my hands sliding down the wall to grasp the top of the headboard.

Seemingly encouraged by my actions, Gavin pressed the tip of his shaft against my opening. Another round of wetness coated my sheath and he moaned, pushing his crown further into me. Larger than I'd expected, he stretched me to the fullest then stilled for a moment, giving me time to adjust to his size. The only sound, our panting breaths.

At last he started a rhythm, the two of us moving in tandem. The speed and tempo increased, along with the slapping of flesh against flesh. My need for him grew, and another orgasm crested over me. Gavin held me still, his own release pulsing through him, and his tongue, warm and wet, stroked the side of my throat, sending delicious shivers down my spine.

His fangs, with their hard, extended length, scraped across my skin and penetrated into the soft spot between my shoulder and my neck. Fevered and dizzy, the most unexpected surge of pleasure rippled through me, spinning my orgasm faster and faster with each tug on my throat.

At long last, my body trembled with my final release. As Gavin withdrew his fangs, he placed tender kisses along the wound. My legs quivered from my loss of blood and my illness. Lightheaded, my vision pinpointed until the darkness took me under.

CHAPTER 12

LEXI

"*A*lexandra, wake up." Gavin's worried voice infiltrated into my mind. He seemed so far away, but I hung on to his words as if they were a life raft and I was adrift at sea.

A comforting and familiar warmth spread around my shoulders. The briefest hint of light penetrated through my eyelids, bringing me from the dark abyss. I opened my eyes.

Gavin's breath eased from him in a rush. "Alexandra, thank God, you're all right."

Seated next to me on his large bed with his arm wrapped around me, he tugged me close, my head coming to rest on his chest.

"What happened?" My parched, dry mouth felt like someone had stuffed cotton in there when I wasn't looking.

"You fainted after I..." Gavin stiffened, the muscles in his arms turning rock hard.

Memories flooded my mind—our lovemaking, the explosive

86

orgasm, his bite, darkness. I drew my fingers to my neck and circled the small puncture wounds. "You fed from me and..."

I pulled away to look at him. Lines formed around his eyes, pain etched in the deep marks. "If you'd died, if I'd killed you, I wouldn't be able to live with myself."

He cared for me, perhaps even loved me. My stomach fluttered, warmth spreading inside. "You didn't hurt me. I'm fine, just a little tired, I guess." Even as I spoke the words, a persistent heaviness settled onto my shoulders, threatening to pull me down once again.

"You need something to eat. I asked Max to bring up a tray, some of the food Ester made for you." Gavin planted a kiss on my forehead, tucked the duvet around my hips, then scooted from the bed. He wore a pair of loose sweatpants, ones that accentuated his trim waist and muscular build. With a quickness only a vampire could possess, he tracked to his dresser, opened one of the drawers, and drew out a white button-down shirt, returning to me before I could blink.

"Here, put this on. Max cannot see you naked." His possessive tone sent a small thrill into my chest. He helped me slide first one arm then the other through the sleeves. His warm licorice scent enveloped me, and I inhaled, soaking it up, committing his unique essence to memory. He clasped every button, leaving only the top one free. The shirt hung from me like a tent.

"There, that's much better." He captured my chin in his palm, his thumb rubbing across my cheek. "How do you feel, are you—"

A loud knock on the door reverberated into the room. Gavin rose from the bed. "Door's unlocked. Come in."

The door slid open with a soft squeak. Max, still dressed in his white shirt and dark pants, entered the room, holding a silver tray with a dome. His gaze drew from Gavin to me and back again. His brow furrowed. "You took off your mask."

"Indeed, I did." Gavin approached, taking the tray from Max's grasp. "Thanks, my friend."

My devoted vampire brought me the tray, setting it on the sheet next to me. He lifted the lid. The scent of warm bread, roast beef, and mashed potatoes wafted into the air. My stomach growled even as my mouth watered. I wasn't sure I could keep the food down, despite how good it looked and smelled.

Gavin gripped the fork, dipped the ends into the mashed potatoes, and brought a small portion to my lips. Not wanting to disappoint him, I opened my mouth. He slid the fork inside. The warm potatoes and gravy tasted succulent, and I swallowed the bite.

A slow smile replaced his worry lines. "Very good, Alexandra, very good."

"Is there anything I can get for you?" Max tilted his head.

Gavin gripped my hand, his fingers intertwining with mine. A tingle of awareness raced along my nerves. "What do you need?"

After the dance and the mind-blowing sex, a dry sheen of sweat coated my skin. Even under Gavin's shirtsleeves, goose-bumps prickled along my arms. "A hot shower would be nice."

Max glanced at Gavin. "Would you like me to prepare the shower for—"

Tension radiated in Gavin's stiff posture. "No one but me sets foot in my private bath."

Max lowered his head in deference. "No problem."

Gavin leaned over and gave me a tender kiss, one that made me want to forget all about the shower. When he released me, he stroked my hair, twirling the end of my braid between his fingers. "I have a large Jacuzzi tub with water jets. It will be warm and ready for you in a few minutes. Finish your meal."

My chest tightened at his tenderness and care. "Thank you, I'll do my best."

Gavin strode across the room and into the private bath. The door shut with a soft click. A moment later, the sound of running water echoed from under the door.

Max leaned against the dresser and crossed his arms. "What's really going on here?"

The muscles in my shoulders tensed. "What do you mean?"

"I've been with Gavin for almost a hundred years. He's never taken to a," his gazed tracked to the puncture wound at my neck to Gavin's shirt, "blood courtesan like he has to you. Are you hoping for a big payoff?"

My face heated, blood rising up my throat and into my cheeks. "No, I came here to dance for him and specifically said no payment was necessary."

Max raised an eyebrow. "You're telling me you don't need money? I find that hard to believe. Many human females become blood courtesans out of desperation. Tell me why you became one."

I gripped the comforter, bunching the material in my fist. "That's none of your business."

He tsked. "Quite the contrary. It is my job to protect Gavin from anyone who may be a threat."

"I'm a threat?"

"In case you haven't noticed, Gavin seems to care about you. That makes you dangerous to him and puts you on my radar."

Exhaustion crested over me. I leaned into the pillow propped against the headboard and rubbed my forehead. "How could I possibly be a danger—"

Max rushed across the room and seized my arm.

I inhaled sharply and peered at him.

Anger radiated in his eyes, and I had no doubt he could kill me in a heartbeat. Until that moment, I hadn't taken his 'body-guard' status seriously, but I did now.

A tic formed in his jaw. "Tell me, and don't lie because I'll know."

Adrenaline raced through my veins, fueling my courage. I yanked my arm free, and he let me go. "Fine, I'm sick, and I need the money for treatment."

"What?" Max drew away from me, his stance rigid. "Ill, how?"

A lump formed in my gut, hardened by fear. "I have a tumor in my spine that became cancerous. I needed the money for radiation treatment. Since I'd heard vampires don't get sick like humans do, why does—"

Max inhaled and slapped his forehead. "Who told you that?"

"A friend of a friend, one of the other courtesans."

"That's not entirely true. Vampires can get sick."

Dismay punched me in the gut. "What will happen to him?" I whispered.

Max's brow furrowed. "Our chemistry isn't the same as yours. We aren't as susceptible to human diseases, but we aren't immune either. Past precedence, of which there isn't much, indicates he could contract the disease, go insane, or nothing. You didn't tell him you were sick, did you?"

I shook my head, and dread's cold fingers tightened around my chest. Gavin drank my blood, my tainted, cancerous blood. I wanted to turn back time, never become a blood courtesan. Pain from my coiled fist raced up my arm. I deserved so much worse.

"How much did he drink from you?"

I scrunched my brow. "What?"

He exhaled. "How long, as in, how many seconds?"

"I don't know!"

"Guess."

I closed my eyes, pressing my hands to my temples. Gavin had fed off me while he held me close. I opened my eyes to Max's concerned face. "Maybe fifteen to twenty. Why does it matter?"

"It means he didn't take much of your blood. If he had…" Max rubbed his thumb and forefinger over his forehead. "Well, it's good that he only took a small amount. There's some medicine I can give him that will counteract the effects. I'll sneak it into his red wine. He won't have a clue it's there."

Hot tears stung the back of my eyes. "What can I do?"

"Stay away from him. He's become attached to you. Nothing good can come from further contact."

The echo of running water slowed to a trickle then ceased. My bath was ready.

Max took a step forward and whispered in my ear, "Break it off quick. I'll wait for you in the car to take you home." He retreated to the door then glanced at me one last time. With a quick shake of his head, he pursed his mouth into a thin line. "Don't delay."

As the door clicked shut, I brought my fist to my mouth to hold back the sob.

CHAPTER 13

LEXI

I shoved my leg through my tights and yanked the material up to my knee. My sore ankle twinged in protest, but I ignored the pain. As fast as I could, I thrust my foot through the other leg, pushed away from the bed, and wrenched the leggings to my waist. Where was my leotard?

My gaze darted over the carpet. Poking out from behind the dresser's claw-foot, my pink outfit contrasted with the furniture's dark grain. My shoulders bunched as I hurried forward.

The click of the bathroom door's latch echoed off the wall, stopping me in my tracks.

"Alexandra, what are you doing?" Gavin's rich baritone voice, the one I'd come to love, wrapped around me like a warm, familiar blanket.

I didn't want to look at him, but I couldn't stop myself. His brow furrowed over his eyes, concern etched in their depths. I swallowed and pulled on my resolve. "I'm leaving."

"What?" His attention drew to the bed with the uneaten plate of food before returning to me. A frown twisted his lip. "I don't understand. The bath is ready."

"I have to go, Gavin." My need to escape, get past this as soon as possible, urged me forward. I scooped up my one-piece suit and held it against me as if it were a shield.

He approached with that quick speed of his and gripped my forearm just below the rolled up sleeve of his shirt. His warm fingers tingled my skin. With more tenderness than I deserved, he brushed his fingertips under my chin and gently tugged, forcing me to look at him. "We still have time. Let me wash you, pamper you, and tease you with all the naughty things I planned to do in the bath."

I fought back the sob that threatened to escape. Deep inside, I wanted that more than I cared to admit. I swallowed and tried to step away, my heart screaming in the process. "I can't stay, not anymore."

Gavin refused to release me, his grasp firm, yet gentle around my forearm. "Wait, Alexandra. Give me a chance to fix whatever I did."

He blamed himself. My chest constricted, squeezing my lungs. I yanked my leotard tighter.

"Stay away from him. He's become attached to you." Max's words echoed in my brain.

Max was right. The easiest way was to break it off quick. I'd already put Gavin at great risk. There was no way I'd let it continue. Not wanting to harm Gavin, but knowing what I had to do, I blurted the words that would hurt him the most. "I'm a blood courtesan. I completed my obligation to service you, so now it's time for me to go." My breath hitched on the last word.

He inhaled, the sound loud in the enclosed space. As if I were a piece of rancid meat unfit to eat, he released his hold on my arm and stepped back. "What did you say?"

I raised my chin and, by sheer strength of will, forced away the tears threatening to form. "Last time I was here you paid me for services I didn't render. I completed my end of the arrangement, so the slate is clean. While he was here, Max offered to take me home. He's waiting in the car."

A pained darkness clouded Gavin's features, and his mouth drew into a thin line. "Much like the first time you were here, Alexandra, I don't believe you, not for a moment, not after what we did—"

I held up my hand. "If you thought this was something more, I'm telling you, it's not." The bitter, foul words burned the back of my throat. Before he could reply, I headed for the doorway, my ankle throbbing with each step. When he didn't yell at me, surprise tingled the skin on my arms. Unlike the last two times I'd left, he held his anger in check. Not that it mattered now. I'd never see him again.

I reached the sill, and the sound of metal scraping against wood halted me. I glanced over my shoulder. Gavin placed his mask over his scars and slid the elastic band under his ear. My heart ached for what I'd done to him.

Unable to bear anymore, I hastened through the hallway and down the stairs as fast as my sore ankle would allow. As I passed the library, I remembered my clothing bag so I darted inside and grabbed it. I opened the elastic end and drew out my flats. A sad heaviness weighed on my shoulders. I exited Gavin's home and headed for the car.

I settled myself into the seat. Max peered at me through the rearview mirror. "I take it he's through with you now?"

"You have no worries," I forced my words to remain steady. "He'll never want to see me again."

As the car pulled away from the mansion, I peered at the broken shingles on the roof and the cracks in the brick. Instead of frightening or sad, they seemed more like character lines, ones I'd grown to love. I closed my eyes, and as the tears flowed, I did nothing to stop them.

∼

GAVIN

I watched until the limo's taillights disappeared around the bend then released the curtain pinched between my fingers. A few embers glowed in the fireplace, but the library had a chill it hadn't had a few moments ago. Maybe that was the emptiness in my heart, I wasn't sure.

Alexandra had pushed me away. Her words still slapped at me, ripping open a scar I'd thought had long ago been covered. Why? What had caused the rapid turnaround? I rubbed my chest, the ache still present, still raw.

I'd followed Alexandra down the stairs and into this very room, using my natural ability to hide silently among the shadows. Unaware of my presence I'd read her expression, saw the changing moods reflected in her features—remorse, pain, guilt. She'd hid something, concealed it from me, of that I had no doubt.

The broken slipper propped against the wingback chair's leg caught my attention. I picked it up and ran my fingers over the torn and ragged lace. I fisted my hand, the material bunching in my grip.

If she was in trouble, forced to go to the blood courtesans for some unconceivable reason, I had to help her. The details in her bio indicated her parents died and she needed the money to support herself. It said she was in the 'arts.' That's why I'd requested her, because we shared the same passion.

Somewhere along the way she'd unleashed something deep within me, the ability to care, to love once again, and I couldn't let her go, not yet. Once I uncovered her secret, my only fear was what I would do to whomever or whatever had harmed her.

CHAPTER 14

LEXI

The tink, tink, tink of rain pelting my window infiltrated my senses, waking me. I drew in a long breath, and Gavin's unique scent, musky and dark, eased into my lungs. I still wore his shirt. Unwilling to take it off, I'd left it on when I'd slipped into bed.

I'd never see Gavin again. My chest tightened, and a small sob escaped my lips. I buried my face in my pillow, but that only brought my nose closer to Gavin's shirt collar.

I flung the sheet back and sat up. Bile rose in my throat, and my mouth watered with the telltale sign I might retch. As I stood, my head pounded, and my bedroom spun, the single bedside lamp becoming two. I placed my hand on the wall to steady myself. With each heartbeat, my pulse pounded at my temple.

I stumbled to the bathroom, and my sore ankle protested. Upon reaching the sink, I placed my palms against the cool porcelain rim. *Breathe, just breathe.* I closed my eyes to keep the spinning world at bay and repeated the mantra over and over. After a few minutes, the urge to vomit passed.

I exhaled, a relieved half-laugh easing from my lips. With shaky fingers, I grabbed the plastic cup from the counter. The world no longer reeled, but the chill wracking my body wasn't a fair trade. Somehow, I managed to pour a glass of water and drink a few sips without spilling any. "Score one for the team."

I set the glass down, and my attention drew to the mirror. My skin was splotchy red and dark circles rimmed my puffy eyes. I'd cried for hours until blissful exhaustion had taken me under. No wonder I looked so bad. I turned to leave. My gaze slid to my neck.

Red and inflamed, Gavin's bite marks stood out like a beacon. I brushed my finger over the wound. A bit of wetness coated my skin. I peered at my fingertip expecting to see blood. Instead, a thin clear liquid covered the tip. *Infected.* Last night, Gavin had licked it, sealing the wound. Maybe because I was sick, it hadn't worked. Great, a perfect way to top off how the evening had ended. Perhaps this was my just desserts.

I drew my hand through my hair. When I pulled my fingers away, several strands ripped from my scalp. The throb at my temple intensified. I swallowed, my throat tightening until I struggled to breath.

My gaze drew to the mirror once again. With shaky hands, I stroked my fingers over my head. More strands slid away like straw caught in the breeze. Tears slid over my lashes. Max was right to make me leave. I didn't want Gavin to experience this, too. I prayed the medicine would work on him.

Shivers rippled over my shoulders and down my legs. A cold sweat rose on my skin. I gripped the sink, forcing the basin to bear my weight. Bed, I needed to return to bed. I headed through the doorway, my shoulder knocking against the doorframe. Pain blossomed at the site, but I didn't care. My entire focus was on my destination. I wobbled across the room and made it without falling. After sliding into bed, I tugged the sheet and blanket up to my chin. The shivers continued.

My phone vibrated on the bedside table, the soft buzz filling the room. I groaned and glanced at the clock, 7:32 a.m. With a quick swipe, I snagged it off the table. Caller ID, Miranda.

"Hey." My voice cracked.

"Hi, Lex, good morning. Just checking in. How are you?"

"I'm okay." The lie slid from my lips without a second thought.

"Hmm, not sure if I believe you, but I'll let it go for the moment. How did your evening go with Gavin?"

"He asked me to dance for him." Regret burned at the back of my throat. "Well, let's just say I won't be seeing him again."

Miranda tsked. "Your choice or his?"

"Mine." Yet I wanted nothing more than to return.

"You received enough money from him to cover your expenses, though, right?"

Money. This had all started with my need for the almighty dollar to fund my treatments. Not that it would matter. My chance of survival didn't look good. "Yes, more than I deserved."

A burst of pain radiated from the bite wound. I groaned, unable to stop the sound from escaping my lips.

"Lexi, damn you. What's wrong?"

I rubbed the spot, heated and sore. "I just need some sleep. Have a headache."

"Hell. Do you want me to come over? I have to go to work, but I can stop by later."

"No, no. I'm sure I'll feel better after a nap. I didn't return from Gavin's until late."

The silence on the other end lasted for several seconds. "All right, but I'll come by tomorrow morning to take you to your next appointment."

"Sounds good, see you then." I placed the phone on the table and closed my heavy eyelids. As I drifted to sleep, visions of a man with a smooth, silky touch, a deep, sensual voice, and a silver mask haunted me.

CHAPTER 15

GAVIN

I cradled the phone under my chin and listened to the ring on the other end of the line. After Alexandra had left, I'd stayed up all day trying to sort out the possibilities, even Googling her name, but nothing significant came up. Her father had died in a car accident, but that was something I already knew.

Bong, bong, bong, bong, bong, bong. The grandfather clock's chime echoed down the hallway. Seated in my wingback chair, I stared through the glass panes of my self-imposed prison. Light from the sun's last rays still painted the sky in faint shades of red. Soon, darkness would encompass the night. I tapped my heel against the wood floor, my impatience getting the better of me.

"Answer the phone!" I rose to my feet, fighting the urge to hurl the thing across the room.

"Hello?" A smooth, familiar female voice slid over the airwaves.

"What did you leave out of Alexandra Dixon's file?" I seethed, spittle flying from my lips.

An exasperated sigh came through the phone. "Gavin Morris, a pleasure as always."

"Cut the sarcasm, *Madame* Rouge, it doesn't suit you."

She cleared her throat. "I run a respectable business. I use top-notch methods to vet and acquire courtesans. The details about each one are carefully noted and summarized in the briefing papers. I leave nothing out, and I resent you think otherwise."

The library door's familiar squeak resounded in the room. Max entered, carrying a tray with a glass of red wine. I turned toward the raging fire, the flames spiking from my anger, and focused on my call. "Alexandra's hiding something, I know it."

"If you're not satisfied with her performance, I can offer you some other courtesans, for a discount, of course."

Revulsion made me swallow hard. I didn't want another courtesan. Alexandra, my beautiful little dancer, was the only one for me. "That won't be necessary. Thank you for your time."

Before she could respond, I ended the call.

Max flicked his fingernail against the wine glass's rim. The ping echoed around the room. "I brought your favorite Bordeaux. Perhaps this will sooth your nerves."

I tugged on my cuffs and strode to the bar. "You're a good friend, my man."

He smiled and handed me the glass. "I heard you mention Alexandra. What was that about?"

I swirled the dark red liquid, and the streaks clung to the side of the glass. How I longed to sniff the exquisite wine's aroma. Instead, I took a sip, enjoying the robust blend as it slid down my throat. The sensation wasn't all that different from blood, but nothing could compare to the sweet taste of Alexandra. My fangs elongated at the memory. "I had a brief conversation with Madame Rouge about Alexandra. Her actions last night seemed contradictory to the woman I'd grown to…"

"Care for?" Max placed his elbows on the bar's countertop and peered at me through the mirror.

I took another sip of the wine, stalling. "Did she say anything to you on the ride home last night?"

"No. I ran into her in the kitchen. She seemed distraught and asked me to take her home. During the entire trip, she didn't say a word."

I tensed. My attention flicked to Max's eyes. "She asked you for a ride in the kitchen?"

He blinked. "Yeah. That's what I recall."

I'd followed Alexandra from the moment she'd left my room. A raging anger swelled in my gut, swirling into a tight knot. I set the wine glass on the counter and stared at him. He didn't flinch, but a bead of sweat formed on his forehead. "How long have we known each other, Max?"

His gaze roamed my features, stopping for a moment at my mask before meeting my eye. "Since I found you on the streets of New York, a recent changeling. It was my hands that tended to your burns over the next several days."

"Yes, I remember. We built an empire in real estate then moved to the West Coast. You've been such a loyal friend, so tell me, why do you lie to me now?"

Max pushed away from the bar, his brow furrowing. "For almost a decade, I've prided myself on protecting you, doing whatever it takes to make sure you're safe."

I chuffed. "Safe? From a courtesan?"

"Yes, and if lying is what it takes then so be it."

My pulse rose, blood pumping through my veins at lightning speed. "What do you know about Alexandra?"

Max focused on the half empty wine glass. "You should drink more of that."

"Why?" I studied the contents, as if the liquid might be some kind of toxic brew.

"Because it could save your life." Max's low words turned my blood cold.

My patience ran out. I seized Max's collar and threw him against the bar. My forearm dug into his neck, pinning him in place. The bottles rattled from the impact. "What did you do?"

His mouth opened and closed, but no sound emerged.

I hissed, baring my fangs. "Tell me!"

He held up his hands in surrender.

A twinge of empathy beat at my chest, and I released him.

He leaned against the bar, red flashing through his eyes.

In the past, I might've beaten him to a pulp or even killed him. My, how I'd changed. I ran my hand through my hair. "I'm sorry, Max. You've been very loyal, but when it comes to Alexandra..."

"She means that much to you?"

"She does."

Max rubbed his reddened throat. "The wine contains an enzyme I procured from one of my sources. It has special qualities and should protect you from certain diseases."

A sudden coldness hit me in the chest. "Is Alexandra sick?"

Max nodded. "She has a tumor in her spine that led to spinal cancer, and she has undergone radiation treatment."

My head spun. No, this couldn't be. The red marks and dark coloration, her tiredness, they were all classic signs of radiation. I'd been too caught up enjoying Alexandra's company to notice. Maybe that's why she became a courtesan, to afford the expensive treatments.

"How did you find out?" I whispered.

"She confessed it to me while you were running the bath for her. I convinced her to leave, to protect you. Just so you know, she didn't realize her illness could harm you. She'd heard that vampires don't get sick like humans do."

I marched across the room, grabbed my jacket off the coat rack, and slipped it on. The familiar weight on my shoulders eased the tension building there, at least for the moment.

Max cleared his throat. "What are you doing?"

I ignored his question and, instead, asked one of my own. "Do you know how far the disease has progressed?"

"No, but she looked rather haggard when I saw her, if you ask me."

I wrapped my hand around the wineglass, amazed it had survived the fight with Max, and downed the contents. If there was any chance of saving Alexandra, I needed to be at full strength.

I strode down the hall, past the grandfather clock, and to the front door, resolve urging me onward. With a quick twist of the knob, I yanked on the door handle. The rhythmic chirp of crickets filled the night.

I placed my foot on the sill, the tip of my shoe hanging over the edge. It seemed like such a small step, but in many ways, it was the biggest of my life. I hadn't been outside these walls in over one hundred years.

Sweat coated my brow, and a single drop slid down the side of my face. I swiped it away, irritated at my irrational fear, but the pounding of my heart quickened nonetheless.

Max placed his hand on my arm. "If she means that much to you, go to her."

Resolve and my love for Alexandra fueled my determination. I clamped my jaw and stepped into the night.

CHAPTER 16

LEXI

*S*omething cool and wet tracked across my forehead. I shivered, the tremor traveling from my head to my toes. An odd tugging sensation on my shoulder had me rolling onto my back.

"Lexi, wake up!" Miranda's voice, distant and fuzzy, tripped through my mind.

I opened my eyes, and the blinding light from my bedside lamp pierced through my skull. With a soft moan, I shut my eyelids once again.

"Oh, thank God, you're awake. After our call you had me worried, so I stopped by after work. Good thing I did." Miranda trailed a damp cloth over my chin and down my neck. As the material scraped along my sore, the wound burned, hot and fevered.

I cried out, pushing her away. "Stop, please."

"Look at me." Miranda clutched my arms, her cool fingers a welcome relief against my skin.

A weary heaviness bore down on me and it was all I could do to focus on her. Even as it was, she appeared to have two sets of eyes. "What are you…"

She stroked her fingers over my forehead, and when she pulled away, a clump of hair slid onto the bedspread. Her eyes widened. "Lexi, you have a fever. I'm taking you to the hospital."

"No, no hospital." I shook my head and the room spun.

"The doctor warned you about getting sick. You don't appear to have a cold. What did…" Miranda inhaled. "Lexi, your neck. It looks infected."

My headache returned, pulsing in tune with the wound at my throat. "I don't feel good." With a shove, I tried to push away the covers so I could get out of bed, but I didn't have the strength.

"Oh, no you don't. Stay here. I'm going to—"

The doorbell's loud chime echoed from the hallway.

"I'll see who's here." As Miranda rose, the bed jostled, and my dresser seemed to double the number of drawers.

I closed my eyes, but that only accelerated the spin. A sheen of sweat erupted along my skin, sending another shiver over my shoulders. A pitiful moan escaped my lips.

With each step, Miranda's footfalls echoed against my skull. The creak of the door opening added to the pain. Heated voices rose down the hall. A man's low timbre slid over my nerves, familiar and comforting. My mind swam, drowning in the whirl.

Drained by the pain, the fever, and the infection racing through my body, exhaustion stole my energy. In the back of my mind, I sensed this was an abyss I couldn't return from. Sadness, spurned by the man's smooth voice, filled my chest, adding to my pain. Mercifully, the ache didn't last as blackness claimed me.

~

GAVIN

"Let me see her. Perhaps I can help." I placed my hand on the doorframe and glanced down the hall. Several doors down, an old woman poked her head out of a nearby apartment. Her gray hair, curled in rollers, clung to her scalp like empty rolls of toilet paper.

She placed her finger over her lips. "Shh."

Alexandra's friend, she'd called herself Miranda, let out a long breath and stepped aside. "I shouldn't. You're the reason she has an infection in the first place, but come in."

I crossed the threshold into a small hallway. To the right, a second-hand couch and mismatched chair surrounded a worn coffee table. To the left, a small kitchen table sat in a corner. Foam protruded from a hole in one of the seat cushions. Alexandra was nowhere to be found.

I turned to Miranda. "Where is she?"

Miranda pointed down the hallway. "In bed. Last room on the right."

I sped down the short hall. As I caught my first glimpse of Alexandra, my chest constricted, squeezing the breath from me. Pale and unmoving, my beautiful little dancer seemed as if death had already claimed her.

I bolted to her side and knelt on the floor. My pulse pounded in my ears. I gently squeezed her fingers. "Alexandra." She didn't respond, but her chest rose and fell with her breaths. Relief rippled over my shoulders, and I leaned my forehead on the soft coverlet.

Her long eyelashes graced her cheek, rosy from her fever. Her lips, plump and slightly parted, seemed to beg for my kiss. Sun-bleached locks of hair caressed her shoulders. I grazed my finger over her sweat-dampened forehead. As I pulled away, several golden strands stuck to my fingers.

A lump formed in my throat.

"Is she awake?" Miranda's voice brought me out of my trance. She leaned over my shoulder, concern etched in the lines around her eyes.

"Not yet." I tightened my grip on Alexandra's hand and gave her another squeeze. "Wake up, beauty."

She didn't stir.

The hair at my nape rose. I slid my fingers along her chin and cupped her head in my hand. Wetness coated my skin. My gaze darted to her throat. Red and inflamed, a white puss oozed from the puncture wounds I'd given her.

"You're the reason she has an infection in the first place." Miranda's words from a few moments ago sank into my brain. This was my fault.

I gritted my teeth. Trailing my thumb over Alexandra's bottom lip like I'd done before, I gave her a gentle shake. "Wake up, Alexandra."

Nothing. No response.

Fear's claws, sharp and pointy, scraped down my back.

"Is she dead?" Miranda screamed the words. She darted to the other side of the bed and clasped her friend's arm.

I placed my fingers alongside Alexandra's throat. Years of feeding from women made me acutely aware of the natural beat of a heart. Her thin, erratic pulse fluttered against my skin. "She's alive, but not for long."

Miranda drew away, her hands curling at her sides. "This can't happen, it can't. I'm calling 911." She bolted for the doorway.

I rose to my feet and gripped her around the waist, holding her against me back to front. She squirmed in my grasp. "What are you doing? Let me go!"

"Stop fighting me! I've seen enough death to know she'll die before they arrive. Only I can save her now."

Miranda stilled in my grasp. "What do you mean? T...Turn her into a vampire?"

I ground my teeth and didn't respond.

One of her booted heels cracked against my shin. "You can't do that. Lexi's dream is to dance on the stage. You'd take that away from her. She'd never forgive you."

"That doesn't mean she can't still dance." I whipped her around to face me. "Would you rather she dies?"

Her eyes flicked back and forth as she studied me. My irritating tic flared to life under my eye. I'd vowed never to turn another, yet here I was, prepared to do exactly that. For Alexandra, I would sell my soul.

"I don't believe you." Miranda's words hit me in the chest. "Can't you heal her with a drop of your blood?"

I stepped away. "Look at her. With the stress from her radiation and the cancer, she's too far along for me to heal her with a small amount of my blood. Even now, her breath rattles with the death call. Don't you hear it?"

Her attention flicked to Alexandra, and her mouth quivered. "She sounds so frail. How can you save her by turning her into a vampire?"

"I'll give her a lot of my blood—"

"Yes, you can't get sick like us and that will cure her—"

"You're under the same misconception as Alexandra. It's possible we can catch human diseases, but not necessarily, and our reaction isn't always the same."

"So you're infected, too. How can you help her then?"

"I didn't consume enough of her blood and drank a concoction to negate it."

Miranda studied me for a long moment, assessing me. "Okay, do what you have to do. I can't watch." She scurried from the room, leaving me alone with Alexandra.

I removed my coat and flung it over the chair next to the old wooden dresser. With a new resolve burning in my gut, I unclasped the button at my sleeve and rolled the material to my elbow. I crawled onto the bed and cupped Alexandra's cheek in my palm. Along the edge of my little finger, her pulse beat once, twice, three times before I couldn't sense it any longer.

Remorse thickened inside of me, and my throat tightened. I leaned down and brought my mouth to hers, giving her a tender kiss. When I drew away, her last breath eased from her lips. Pain exploded inside my chest, shattering my heart.

Without a second thought, I bared my fangs and sank them into her throat, piercing the wound I'd created. With long pulls, I drew in her blood, yanking the tainted fluid from her. Swallowing, over and over, I had to clean out the blemish before I gave her my life-saving blood. After I'd taken enough, I eased my fangs from her throat and sealed the wound.

I scraped my fang's sharp tip across my wrist. Blood welled from the gash. Red, dark, and filled with the antibodies that would change her forever, I held my wrist over her mouth. A tiny drop landed on her lip then another. Soon, my blood slid onto her tongue.

Time seemed to slow. I didn't waver from my task, giving her more and more.

At last, I brought my wrist to my mouth and licked the skin, closing the cut.

"Alexandra." My voice broke. How long it took to transform a human into a vampire was unique to each individual. I slid off the mattress, gripped the chair, and drew it next to the bed. As I settled in, all I could do was wait.

CHAPTER 17

LEXI

*T*he drip, drip, drip of the water faucet in the bathroom, the ping of the refrigerator's coils, and the rhythmic sound of Gavin's breaths dragged me from my sleep. How did I know those were Gavin's breaths? I wasn't sure, but deep inside, I recognized him. My mind whirred at the thought, and I opened my eyes.

Seated next to me, Gavin smiled, the curve of his lip creating that adorable dimple I'd grown to love. Confusion tugged at the back of my mind. "Where's Miranda? She was here—"

"Your friend received a call that her mother fell and broke her hip. She went to the hospital and told me to tell you to relax and take it easy. How do you feel?"

I blinked. No fever, no headache, no fatigue. I brought my hand to my throat and brushed my fingers over Gavin's bite mark. Instead of the inflamed, jagged wound, my skin was smooth, not even the hint of a scar. "I feel okay, I guess."

A relieved breath eased from him. "That's good, very good indeed."

My heart tripped. Gavin never left his home. "What are you doing here?"

Gavin's features turned stoic, his mouth drawing into a thin line. "Do you think I'd let you walk out like that? My beautiful little dancer, I had to see you."

My cheeks heated, memories of what transpired between us and my bitter words flooding my mind. Needing time to process my thoughts, I swiped my hand through my hair. Fine blonde strands came away in my fingers. Tears pricked behind my eyes. "How can you call me that? Look at me." I held up my hair. "I'm anything but beautiful."

A mixture of sadness and warmth radiated in Gavin's brown eye. "You are and will always be beautiful to me."

My chest expanded, filling with his kind words. Gavin cared for me for who I was, not what I looked like. If I wasn't careful, I'd let him back inside and that was something I could never do. My gaze slipped to the bedspread.

Gavin grasped my fingers and brought them to his lips, giving them a tender kiss. "Besides, your hair will grow back, I promise."

Before I could stop myself, my attention drew to his features. "Grow back?" I blinked, trying to comprehend his words.

"You feel great, better than you have in a long time. Your infection is gone and your wound healed. It won't be long before your hair regrows as well."

"How?"

His shoulders tensed. The familiar tic, the one that indicated he wasn't happy, pulsed under his eye.

A chill started at the base of my neck. "Tell me."

He swallowed and met my gaze. "You are no longer human."

Blood rushed to my ears, drowning out his words. I tugged my hand from his grasp. "I'm a vampire?"

His brow furrowed, a crease forming in the skin along the

edge of his mask. "You died. The infection was more than your body could handle so I—"

"Took matters into your own hands and changed me. Just like that." I snapped my fingers and scooted across the bed, putting some distance between us. "You didn't give me a choice. I told you I didn't want to become a vampire."

He rose, knocking his chair over in the process. The back crashed against the bedside table and landed on the carpet with a thud. "Alexandra."

"You said you'd never change another against their will. Why did you do it?" My pulse pounded, hard and fast.

"Because I didn't want to go on without you." His heartfelt words beat against my soul, breaking down the walls, but I'd already put him at risk with my disease, and I couldn't forgive myself.

I slid from the bed, the mattress a barrier between us. It might as well have been an ocean. "Gavin, did you drink from me tonight?"

He pursed his mouth, his lack of response all the answer I needed.

My scalp tingled. "How much?"

He studied me, a warm glint forming in his eye. "As much as I could before I gave you my blood."

I bit my lip, fear for him squeezing my insides. "I have, er, had spinal cancer. I thought vampires couldn't get sick like humans. I was wrong. If I had known, I never would've become a blood courtesan."

"If you hadn't become a courtesan, I never would've met you."

I fisted my hand and brought it to my lips. "You drank too much, you could get sick. You shouldn't have changed me."

"For you, I'd do it again in a heartbeat." He edged around the end of the bed, coming closer.

Tears rimmed my eyes, blurring my vision. I couldn't bear what I'd done to him, what he'd done to me. Anger, frustration, love, all rolled together into a tight ball in my gut. Before I could change my mind and run into his arms, find the solace I craved, I turned my back on him. "Don't come any closer. I can't deal with this, with any of it."

He clasped my shoulders, the strength in his grip seeping through his shirt, the one I still wore. Tears spilled over my lashes. "Gavin, please, just go."

"Alexandra," his grip tightened for a moment before he released me, "I don't want to leave you here alone, not after what you've been through. There's much you need to know about becoming a vampire."

"Go, now!" I whirled on him and shoved at his chest. To my shock, he flew across the room and slammed into the wall. Bits of plaster floated from the ceiling. I gasped and raced to his side. "Gavin, I'm sorry."

Before I could blink, he tugged me against him and brought his lips to mine, giving me a bruising kiss. The passion ignited between us, and I melted under his onslaught. I loved him, cared for him, deeply. Even so, he'd drunk from me, putting himself at great risk, and changed me into a vampire against my will. I couldn't be around him. After breaking the kiss, I stepped away, my heart shattering in the process.

"Please, leave, just go." I shook my head, the tears streaming down my cheeks.

A pain I'd never seen before etched itself in the lines around his eye. He swallowed, his Adam's apple undulating in his throat. "Alexandra, I'll give you some time to think, to calm down, but this isn't over between us. I will return, that, I promise."

Before I could respond, he left. After he disappeared down the hallway and the front door's latch clicked, I crumpled to the carpet and sobbed.

CHAPTER 18

GAVIN

*U*sing my vampire speed, the trip home from Alexandra's apartment took minutes. Now I stood in the entryway, my fingers clasped around the door handle. The morning sun brightened the sky, and the stars no longer twinkled. Instead, a deep purple hue covered the heavens. The hair at my nape prickled. My grasp tightened around the knob, but I didn't go inside, not yet.

A part of me longed to stay rooted in place and let the sun fry me until I screamed from the agony. The physical pain would be much easier than the torment that wracked my soul. Alexandra's rejection still burned deep inside. I clamped my jaw, and an ache radiated up my cheek and along the scar line.

To save her, I broke my strongest commitment never to turn another against their will. The door knob disintegrated in my palm, my grip too much for the metal. Shards scattered across the welcome mat and down the cobblestone steps.

I shoved open the door and strode inside. The emptiness,

something I'd never noticed before, wrapped around me like a cocoon. Yet instead of the comfort it once provided, the place seemed devoid of emotion, devoid of life.

My gaze tracked to the library door. I sprinted down the hallway, my boots echoing off the walls. As I walked into the large room, I halted. My breath heaved in and out of my lungs. Like an old movie, I imagined Alexandra dancing for me, pirouetting across the floor, her pink ballet slippers whisper quiet against the polished wood. Beauty radiated from her in every twirl, every plié, every arabesque, her love for dance evident in each move.

When she'd left here last, the bitterness in her words had cut me deep. Despite my desire to lash out, I'd held in my anger and kept my promise. Even tonight, after she'd tossed me out of her apartment, the old need to snap at her hadn't appeared. Something changed inside me. Goosebumps formed on my arms.

I'd opened myself to her, shared my past and my pain. The way she'd caressed my scar, understanding and respect etched around her eyes, had bonded me to her in more ways than I wanted to admit. Tonight, I'd made her another promise, one that I'd return. Conviction coiled in my gut, fueling my determination. I'd honor that vow, no matter the consequences or outcome. If she rejected me still, so be it.

A low humming noise rang in my ears, loud enough to send a spike of pain behind my eyes. Perspiration beaded along my brow. I shook my head and headed for the bar.

I wrapped my hand around a bottle of merlot situated in the small wine rack and pulled it out. After removing the metal stopper, I poured the liquid into a glass. The soft glugging of the wine as it slipped from the bottle should've registered on my senses, but I couldn't hear anything above the ringing in my ears.

The headache, the sweat, the increasingly loud ping inside my head could only mean one thing. I was sick. The cancer would work its magic on me, but whether I contracted the disease itself or go insane from the tainted blood remained to be seen.

The medicine Max had given me eradicated the small amount of blood I'd first consumed from Alexandra, but with as much as I took to save her, no amount of medicine could eliminate it all. At least the medicine had flowed from me to Alexandra, helping cure her of her disease as she went through the change from human to vampire. Funny how different substances supercharged during the transition. Medicine was one that often did. Whether the remaining antibodies in my vampire blood would win out was anyone's guess, but I wouldn't go down without a fight.

Someone placed their hand on my shoulder.

I jerked. The wineglass tipped over, the red liquid following a crack along the edge of the bar. With the quickness of my species, I gripped the person's hand and twisted it behind their back, pinning them against me back to front.

The familiar cut of Max's blond hair and his impeccable suit made me pause. I pushed him away. "What are you doing?"

He furrowed his brow, his blue gaze assessing me. "Didn't you hear me? I asked how it went with Lexi."

His words, muffled and faint, penetrated through the fog in my brain. I shook my head. The vibration heightened my irritation. "I screwed up, Max, changed Alexandra without her consent. She kicked me out."

"You did what?" Max's mouth moved, but the words slipped by as if on a breeze, undecipherable. Good thing I'd read his lips.

"She died in my arms, but I cleaned out her blood and gave her some of mine. Thanks to you and your medicine, my blood was untainted." Pain pounded at the back of my skull. I gritted my teeth.

His lips moved, but I couldn't decipher his words. As he approached me, his mouth pulled into a thin line. He gripped my arm and drew me away from the bar.

Anger flared at my temple. The pain in my head exploded. I yanked my arm from his grasp. Before I could stop myself, I grabbed one of the barstools and threw it at him. "Leave me alone!"

He ducked as the stool flew past. It crashed against the bar's mirror. Glass shards scattered across the polished wood floor. A small shaft of sunlight penetrated through the crack between the thick curtains. It lit up the floor's surface like a spotlight on a dance floor. Dust filtered through the beam, but there was no dancer. Heaviness settled onto my chest, my heart aching.

"I will return, that, I promise." Spurned by the madness claiming my mind, my vow to Alexandra tormented me on a cellular level, becoming a part of every fiber in my being.

I had to see her. Now.

Before Max could stop me, I bolted for the hallway. As I ran toward the front door, I sensed Max pursuing me.

I gripped the door handle and twisted the knob. Max barreled into me, pinning me against the wood. A surge of energy burst through my veins. With a hard shove, I flung him off my back.

He hit the wall and slid to the floor. Stunned but not out, he'd recover soon. Now was my chance.

I focused on the door. The two doorknobs made my head spin. I stretched for one, but instead of the cool metal, my fingers skimmed the door's wooden surface. As I reached for the other, a sharp pain bloomed at the back of my skull. My vision brightened for a moment then I passed out.

CHAPTER 19

LEXI

A ray of sunlight streamed through the glass over the top of the kitchen window's curtain. The light tracked a line across the table, and I slid the tip of my finger into the shaft. An agony I'd never experienced before, one far worse than the tumor I used to have, rippled up my arm. I jerked my hand away. Smoke rose into the air along with the scent of my burning flesh. As I studied my finger, the skin healed, and the tissue turned from red to pink to my natural pale tone.

Given the intense pain, I couldn't fathom the torment Gavin must've experienced to cause irreparable scars. A swell of empathy struck me in the chest. *Don't cry, don't cry, don't cry.* I'd done enough of that already.

After Gavin had left, I'd taken a shower, eager to wash away the sweat coating my body. Most of my hair at the back of my head had fallen out along with several lengths over one ear. In its place was a thin layer of fuzz, fine like a newborn's. I looked like a strange baby chick. The dark wig on the table, the one Miranda had promised to acquire, taunted me, but I couldn't bring myself to put it on.

Unable to sleep, I'd spent much of the day reading past posts in the private Blood Courtesans' Facebook group. I'd learned a lot about what it meant to be a vampire. Obvious differences like not going out in the sun, added strength and speed, the need to drink blood to survive, and living for nearly an eternity I'd already figured out on my own. The shattered salt shaker I'd played with was a good testament to that.

What I'd discovered, though, was that some vampires had the ability to move objects, create fire from their fingertips, or blend into the shadows. I could get used to that, but I was still upset at losing my opportunity to dance. Even if I'd landed the job at the Oregon Ballet Theater, rehearsals were in the afternoon. Fat chance I'd make it there given my new circumstances. I'd never realize my dream. Heavy and unwanted, sadness weighed me down.

I wiped my palms against my jeans and glanced at the clock—5:32 p.m. The second hand ticked past the one and toward the two, the sound reverberating off the walls. I wiped my hand over my face, my thoughts returning to Gavin against my will. He'd taken my blood, drank it without knowledge of the disease racing through my veins.

I pushed away from the table, the chair leg scrapping against the floor. With quick strides, I paced the room. Had Max given Gavin more of the medicine? Would it work? I reached for my phone for what seemed like the thousandth time today, the urge to call him tingling my fingertips. My hand hovered over the screen, but I couldn't do it.

After Gavin changed me against my will, and the way I'd treated him, kicking him out like a stray dog, I didn't know what was up and what was down, nor how to make things right.

The clink of a key inserting into the front door and the

squeak of the knob turning resounded. My pulse quickened. *Gavin?* I raced down the hall.

As the front door swung open, Miranda's eyes widened. She cradled a box under one arm. The cardboard slid from her grasp, but she caught it before the package hit the ground. "Lexi!"

She tugged me into her embrace. "I'm so glad to see you."

My eyes turned hot and gummy, and I held her close, thankful she was in my life. "How's your mom?"

"Settled and scheduled to transfer to rehab in a few days. I'm sorry I had to leave. Did Gavin tell you she broke her hip?"

I nodded.

Miranda leaned forward and gripped my hands in hers. "God, I hated to leave." She sniffed. "I thought you were dead from that infection. Tell me what happened. Did Gavin change you?"

Wrapping my fingers around hers, I drew her down the hall. "Come in the kitchen."

We reached our favorite gathering place, and she plopped into one of the chairs, dumping the box on the table. "Okay, Lex, tell me."

I slid in the seat next to her and placed my hand on hers. "I'm a vampire."

Miranda's mouth parted. Her gaze roamed over my features, stopping for a moment at my lips before returning to my eyes. "How do you feel about that?"

A uneasy heaviness settled onto my shoulders. With a long exhale, I drew my hand away and stood, sure that pacing the room would ease some of the tension. "Gavin bit me, drank a lot of my blood, then gave me some of his, changing me."

"Well, that's a good thing, right? You're alive and—"

I whirled on her, my guilt twisting my gut into a tight coil. "No, it's not. What you told me Leslie said, that vampires don't get sick like we do, isn't always true. By drinking my blood, I put Gavin's life at risk. I'll never forgive myself if something happens to him."

121

Miranda rose from her chair and approached me. Regret reflected in her blue eyes. "I'm so sorry. I believed what Leslie said."

I tugged my friend into my arms. "It's not your fault. She may have believed it herself."

Miranda pulled back and peered at me. "What are you going to do?"

"I don't know. I'd hoped the radiation treatments would work and I'd dance again someday. I lost my dream when Gavin changed me and exposed him to a disease in the process."

"I'm sorry, Lex." She glanced behind her to the table. "Maybe this will warm your spirits. In all the commotion, I forgot to tell you. When I arrived yesterday to check on you, I ran into the UPS delivery guy outside your apartment complex. He couldn't get the manager on the intercom, and I noticed your name on his package."

My gaze tore to the box on the table.

"I told him I'd take it to you since that's where I was headed. He didn't want to give it to me at first, but he caved when I gave him my best smile."

I grinned. "I'll bet he did."

"I was halfway up the stairs when I realized I didn't have your wig. So I returned to my car." She glanced at the floor before returning her attention to me. "In the process of snagging your new hairdo, I forgot the box. I'm sorry."

I gave her arm a gentle squeeze. "You have no reason to be sorry. I'm thankful to have a friend like you."

As she smiled, the setting sun's rays lit up her dark hair. I swear the fine strands glowed like a halo.

"Open it," she whispered, enthusiasm dripping from her tone.

I turned toward the package. My name and address, emboldened in black ink, marked the paper. The sender's information was absent. Was the parcel from Gavin? I had to know.

With hope that I didn't dare acknowledge, I placed my hands

on the parcel and picked it up. From what I could tell, the box weighed about two pounds. I ripped the paper off and lifted the lid.

Inside, a pair of gorgeous pink ballet slippers lay nestled in tissue. A small notecard rested amid the laces, the words—*To my beautiful little dancer*—printed on the front. The back of my throat tightened as my breath caught.

Miranda peered over my shoulder. "Those are nice. Gavin, right?"

Words couldn't get past the lump in my throat, so I nodded.

I set the box on the table and grasped the card. The envelope's smooth and elegant parchment teased my fingers. With the lump in my throat growing by the second, I flipped open the corner and slid out the piece of paper.

Alexandra, through your zest for life, your love of dance, and your remarkable empathy, you awakened something within me I thought no longer existed—the desire to share another's company. I've found that with you. Please give me another chance to show you what you've come to mean to me. Gavin

As the card slipped from my fingers, my eyes misted, and the letters blurred. The sincerity in his words beat at the chains around my heart, breaking the links one by one. I'd never been happier than when I'd danced for Gavin.

My phone buzzed in my back pocket. Using the distraction to cover my reaction to Gavin's note, I drew the device from its usual home. Unable to decipher the caller ID through my tears, I swiped my finger across the screen anyway. "Hello?"

"Alexandra Dixon?" a man's low voice filtered over the line. Familiarity pricked the back of my mind, but I couldn't quite place him.

"Yes, who is this?"

Miranda sat in one of the kitchen chairs and drew one of the ballet slippers from the box. The laces dangled over her wrists as if reaching for the floor, eager to perform.

"Max. I'm calling about Gavin."

A flush of adrenaline tingled through my limbs. "Is he all right?"

Max cleared his throat.

My senses went on high alert. Miranda stopped her examination of the slippers and peered at me. "What's the matter?" she mouthed.

"My deepest apologies. I was wrong to send you away. Gavin needs you."

Blood drained from my face, and I plopped into the chair next to my best friend. "Is he sick?"

"He's losing his mind and is on a rampage, destroying—" A loud crash, like metal against wood echoed over the line. "Crap, there went part of the bookcase."

My heart skipped a beat before pounding double time. "He drank my blood. I was out of it, dying, and didn't get a chance to warn him about my disease."

Max exhaled. "He already knew you had spinal cancer. I told him. I gave Gavin the medicine like we'd discussed, so it was in his blood when he came to see you. After he bit you, the medicine turbocharged during your transition from human to vampire. That's why you survived."

"Gavin knew." A jolt rippled down my arms. He drank my blood even though he must've understood the consequences. Love for him tightened my chest to the point of pain. "What can I do?"

Another loud crash reverberated from Max's end of the phone. "I gave him more medicine, and I think it's helped to a point, but what he really needs to stave off the madness is for someone he cares about to be by his side, help him through it, ground him. I can only do so much."

Understanding hit me like a hammer to the head. Max thought I could save Gavin. I swallowed, forcing the lump from the throat. "You want me to come over?"

"I'd come get you myself, but I must stay here, make sure he doesn't harm himself or try to leave. I can send a cab, if you'd like."

"I'll take you." Miranda gripped my arm. "Sorry, but I can hear Max over the line, as well as the wreckage."

I could run to Gavin, but I didn't trust my new vampire skills yet. After wrapping my arm around her shoulder, I hugged my best friend. "Thank you."

"You're welcome," she whispered.

Pulling away, I cleared my throat and concentrated on Max. "No need to call a cab. I have a ride. We'll be there as soon as possible."

"Perfect. I'll contain him until you arrive." He cut the connection.

Outside the window, the sky darkened. A soft ping resonated in my chest. Deep inside, I understood the sun had set.

Miranda drew her keys from her pocket and shook them. "I'm ready if you are."

The jingle, so innocent and mundane, brought tears to my eyes. Blinking them away, a resolve built from the depths of my soul. I grabbed my coat off the back of the chair, shoved my phone in the left pocket, and headed down the hallway. Gavin had risked his life to save mine. I would do everything in my power to bring him back from the edge.

CHAPTER 20

LEXI

J took several long, deep breaths, willing my nerves to calm, but it didn't work. Instead, I tapped the toe of my flats against the car's speaker, the rhythmic pounding in synch with my erratic pulse.

"If you break my speaker with your new strength, I'll expect you to buy me a new one." Miranda glanced at me before returning her gaze to the road.

"Sorry," I mumbled and forced my foot to remain still. My finger picked up the cadence in its place, and drummed it against the arm rest. "What if we don't get there in time?"

"Don't borrow trouble." Miranda's words slid through my mind, pricking a memory of what Danae, the tarot card reader, had said. *"Trouble may lay ahead with illness or misfortune."* I let loose a short exhale. How about both?

The streets of Portland, lined with trees wrapped in bright white lights for the upcoming holidays, sped by in a blur. As far as I was concerned, we couldn't get there fast enough.

Next to my hip, my phone vibrated in my coat pocket. Adrenaline flew across my nerves, tightening my shoulders. Fingers shaking, I slid my phone from its resting place. Caller ID—Oregon Ballet Theater.

I blinked. It had been weeks since I'd auditioned with them for the temporary job. Since I hadn't heard back about the position, I'd written them off. With a swipe of my finger, I answered, "Hello?"

"Alexandra?" a woman's smooth voice asked.

"Yes, this is her." I almost choked on the words.

"This is Rachel Warfield. You auditioned with us a few weeks ago for one of the temporary jobs in our theater. I'm sorry we didn't get back to you sooner. Our hiring manager had a death in the family and was away for an extended time."

"Please give him or her my condolences."

"Well, my manager was very impressed with your performance. If you're still interested, we'd like to offer you a position as backup to the lead female." Rachel's tone softened. "Since she recently announced she's pregnant, we anticipate the role could expand to you becoming the lead. The one caveat is that we need you to come in tonight to practice with the troupe. I know it's short notice, but we had a lot of applicants and we're in a bind. Can you join us? If you can't, we need to move on to the next person on the list."

"Keep trying, kiddo, you never know when you'll catch your big break." My father's words pinged across my mind. He'd wanted this for me for so long. My dream, my chance to become a ballerina on the live stage, was within my grasp.

Funny how timing was everything. I bit the side of my cheek, indecision swirling in my gut for all of an instant. That was all it took. I made up my mind. "I'm sorry. I can't come in tonight. If it were any other night, I would."

"I'm sorry to hear that. Well, perhaps another opportunity will arise."

"Thank you, and good luck in filling the position." I ended the call and waited for disappointment to wash over me, but all I noticed was a sense of peace.

"You must love him." Miranda's sentiment filled the space between us.

Brimming with hope, for him, for us, my chest lightened. "I do. Very much."

Trees lined the road, their tall spires pointing toward the stars. I leaned my forehead against the glass and peered into the night sky. My life had changed so much over the past few weeks. It was all due to Gavin. A twinge, of faith perhaps, burst from deep inside, overflowing with courage and determination I hadn't known I'd possessed.

As we rounded the bend, the mansion's lights lit up the entryway. With its cracked brick, the place seemed like home now. Miranda slowed, and I didn't wait for the car to stop. Instead, I opened the door and bolted up the stone steps.

"Gavin?" My breathless words echoed down the long hall.

The library door opened and Max emerged from the room. He headed toward me, his brow furrowed. "Lexi, I'm glad you're here."

I met him next to the grandfather clock. The ticking of its inner workings eased inside me, calm and steady.

He took my hand, his fingers shaking. "Lexi, I'm afraid Gavin's in bad shape. I may have underestimated how fast the madness progressed. I'm not sure you should see him."

My adrenaline spiked, but I used the fear to bolster my determination. "Where is he?"

Max studied me for a long moment then tilted his head down the hallway. "He's in the library."

"Thanks, Max. He won't hurt me. I know it."

Max nodded once. "He loves you. Use that to bring him back."

"Lexi!" Miranda ran up the steps. The bang of the door hitting the wall carried down the hallway.

"Miranda, I'm headed to the library to help Gavin." I jerked my head at Max. "Wait here with Max."

She nodded. "Be careful."

I gave her a quick, reassuring smile. "I will."

As I approached the library, a crash echoed from the room, the sound of wood splintering unmistakable. I gripped the handle and pushed open the door. I gaped at the scene that greeted me.

Broken in several places, one of the wingback chair's legs protruded from its cushion, as if the thing had been impaled. Bits of glass from the oak bar's mirror scattered across the floor and reflected the light from the fire roaring in the fireplace, the shards shimmering like diamonds.

Gavin stood next to the window, shoulders hunched, his breath coming in great heaves. He glanced my way, and his eye glowed red. Without his mask, his scar pulled tight across his features, but his strength, his determination, and all that he'd overcome filled me with a sense of respect and pride.

"Get out." His dark tone skated across the room.

I took a step forward. "Gavin, it's me, Alexandra."

His fingers curled around the Stradivarius's neck, the strings dangling from the end. What remained of the belly lay broken and scattered at his feet. He'd loved that instrument, almost as if it had been a part of him. Tears pricked my eyes, but my conviction didn't waver.

"Gavin, don't you recognize me?" I inched forward, treating him as if he were a large predator trapped in a cage. In many ways, that's what he had been until he'd broken through the chains holding him to save me. I wouldn't give up on him.

A feral growl burst from his lips, halting me.

He tossed what was left of his precious violin against the wall. The wood shattered, raining down on the floor with a loud crash. He slammed his hands together and cracked his fingers. "Get out!"

"No!" I edged closer and held my ground. "Let me help you, Gavin. I care for you."

A tic started in his jaw, but the lines around his eye softened. "No one cares for me."

"I do, more than you know." I took another step forward, my gaze never wavering from his.

His good eye flashed red and another untamed growl emerged from his mouth.

Even though I tensed, I knew deep inside that he loved me. I held out my hand, palm up. "Come back to me, Gavin. Fight this. I know you can. I believe in you."

The rumble died on his lips. His features contorted, the muscles in his face trembling as if his struggles were as much internal as external. Unable to stay away any longer, I crossed the distance between us and slid my arms around him, pressing my head against his chest.

A tremble rattled through him, the shiver so violent it travelled between us and settled into my bones. He gripped my arms, his fingers digging into my flesh. Pain rippled down my skin, but I refused to cry out. Instead, I rubbed his back, trying to ease the tension in his muscles.

"You're sick, Gavin. The tainted blood you drank worked its way into your mind. Concentrate on me, on the sound of my voice and return to me."

An anguished moan rumbled in his chest. "I don't deserve you."

"You're a good man. You risked your life, this very illness, all for me. To do that for another makes you more than worthy."

He tugged me away enough to look me in the eyes. Pain and torment radiated in his gaze, but in the depths of his brown eye sparked hope, belief that it could be so. "Alexandra?"

I let loose a relieved exhale. "Yes, Gavin, I'm here."

He released his iron-clad grip on my arms, closed his eye, and swayed on his feet. I stiffened my legs and grasped his shirt, doing all I could to steady him. The material bunched between my fingers. He regained his balance, and a glimmer of clarity sparked in his eye. Tenderly, he brushed his fingers over the peach fuzz hair covering the back of my head.

A bead of sweat slid along the edge of his mask, and like before, I trailed my finger over his skin, wiping away the moisture. "Gavin, in your note, the one you sent with the lovely slippers, you said you wanted to share your company with me. That meant more to me than you know. I want to be with you."

He blinked and shook his head. "Keep talking…"

Emboldened with hope, I let the words flow, speaking whatever came to my mind. "You've been the most aggravating vampire I know. You're the only one I know, well, except for Max, but every time I stepped foot in your home, you drove yourself further into my heart. Now, there's no going back for me. You are as much a part of me as I am. I love you, Gavin."

"Alexandra…" The tendons in Gavin's neck stood out, and the tic in his jaw pulsed with tension. Sweat poured off his brow. With a soft moan, he gripped my waist and held on as if I were his lifeline.

I wrapped my fingers around his neck and brushed my lips against his. He tugged me to him. Taking control, he deepened the kiss and slid his tongue along the sensitive seam of my lips. I opened to him, inviting him in. He devoured me, his hunger driving into a frenzy. Since I was no longer human, my heightened senses intensified every sensation. I dug my nails into his scalp, holding him there, letting him know I wanted him as much as he wanted me.

His erection grew firm and long, pressing against my hip. A shiver of need and desire so strong rippled along my nerves. My fangs extended, and I nipped the inside of his lip, drawing blood.

He moaned, his teeth lengthening in response, and he grazed the pointy tip along my tongue before breaking the kiss. With that familiar tenderness, he gripped my face is his palm. His breaths, long and slow, caressed my cheek. We stayed that way for several moments. At last, he broke the silence. "You brought me back from the brink of madness. Thank you."

My breath hitched. "You wouldn't be in this situation if it wasn't for me. Draining me of that tainted blood, you knew you could get sick or go mad—"

"And I'd do it again, for you, my Alexandra." He smiled and kissed the end of my nose. "I love you, too."

"You understood my babbling?"

"Every word." His eye gleamed with delight. "Stay with me. Forever."

"What?"

"Stay with me here, in this mansion." He glanced around the room. "I'll even let you redecorate it."

I choked, happiness filling my heart. "What if I want something chic and new, maybe from Pottery Barn?"

His deep laughter reverberated off the walls. "If that's what your heart desires, then so be it."

I glanced down, not wanting him to see my tears. Broken pieces of the Stradivarius caught my attention. "Your violin."

His brow furrowed and sadness formed in the lines around his eyes then he brushed his lips over mine. "It's just wood and string. Beautiful Alexandra, what's important is I have you."

My chest expanded, filling with a deep, profound love like I'd never experienced before. *"What you think you want may not be what you need."* Danae, the tarot card reader, was right when she'd said a man, a strong and opinionated authority figure, would have a significant impact on my life. Gavin had changed everything for me, giving me a love I'd longed for and chased away my fears.

I leaned close and whispered in his ear, "You were right. You taught me to love the word 'beautiful,' and I am...your *beautiful* little dancer."

CHAPTER 21

LEXI

Two months later...

I placed the bottle of merlot in one of the empty slots in the enormous walk-in wine bar and skimmed my finger along the metal casing. With its glass door showcasing the fine selection of wines, the designers at Cantoni had done an excellent job. I shook my head as I smiled, a few strands of my hair, now grown in, caressing my cheek.

My attention flicked around the room, my gaze landing on Gavin's large frame. The tips of his dark hair cascaded over the collar on his jacket, and his muscles tightened under his button-down shirt, pulling taut against his broad back. The urge to run my hands over him tingled my fingers.

He glanced at me. A smile tugged at his lip, creating that dimple I'd grown to love so much. Happiness threatened to explode in my chest.

"I recognize that look. What are you up to?" He drew a wine

glass from its box and set it on the hand-carved bar. Half of a large tree cut lengthwise, the donor was a gorgeous cedar, harvested from the coast range and polished to a magnificent gloss.

I shrugged, feigning ignorance.

He strode across the room, confidence and determination lining his features. With a quick tug, he drew me against him. My hands landed on his chest. "Come now, Alexandra, you can't hide things from me. Might as well confess to it now."

I trailed my fingers into his scalp, enjoying how a few strands of his dark, silky hair tickled the back of my hand. "I bought something."

He chuckled. "When I said you could redecorate, I had no idea what that would entail."

"Aren't you happy with how it turned out?" I brushed my finger along the soft scars on his cheek.

"No, but I didn't think you'd toss out all my antiques."

"Well, I think you'll like this one." A zip of adrenaline coursed through my veins. I pushed out of his arms. "Over here."

I crooked my finger, encouraging him to follow.

He pursed his lips, but did as I asked. When we reached the console table under the large picture window, I opened one of the doors and withdrew a package.

"Here, this is for you." I placed the box in his arms and took a step back.

His brow rose, and his attention flicked from me to the bright pink package and back again. "A gift for me? Why?"

I stifled a giggle. "Because it's your birthday, and oh, maybe, just maybe, because I love you."

His features softened, a smile tugging at his lip once again. "You love me? That's good to know, and you couldn't possibly love me as much as I love you."

I trailed my fingers over his bicep, enjoying the steel beneath his shirt. "Open the present."

Warmth radiated in his gaze. "It's been years since I've celebrated my birthday."

"Well, it's high time you did." I pointed to the box cradled in his arms. "Go ahead. Open it. I wrapped it in your favorite color."

"Noted." His tone held a hint of amusement. Without further delay, he placed the package on the table and ripped the wrapping paper. The tearing sound echoed off the walls.

A sudden nervousness trickled along my nerves, and I bit my lip.

The box finally free of its wrapping paper, Gavin lifted the lid. My heart stuttered.

His gaze rose to meet mine. "Where did you get this?"

"Max found it. I wasn't sure if you'd like it. It's not a Stradivarius, but it's—"

Gavin cupped my chin in his palm and kissed me. A thrilling warmth spread through my body, lighting up my nerves in all the right places. Breaking the kiss, he brushed his fingers through my short hair and stared into my eyes. "My beautiful little dancer. I absolutely love it and will cherish the violin always."

My phone buzzed in my jeans pocket. I exhaled, my shoulders slumping. "Timing is everything, isn't it?"

A smirk toyed at Gavin's lip.

Not bothering to look at the caller ID, I swiped my finger across the screen. "Hello?"

"Alexandra Dixon?" a man's voice carried over the line.

I straightened my back, curiosity piquing my interest. "Yes?"

"My name is Harrison Cross. I own a new dance troupe catering exclusively to the burgeoning vampire community in the Portland metropolitan area. A friend of mine recommended you as the lead in my upcoming production, a rendition of *Swan Lake*. Would you be interested in the part? No audition necessary."

I opened my mouth, but nothing came out. My lungs didn't seem to want to work. I peered at Gavin.

The smirk turned into a full-fledged grin. He inclined his head. "Well, are you going to answer him?"

I blinked. Somehow, Gavin had scored me the position I'd craved for so long, but I'd wanted to do this on my own, not have it bought for me. I concentrated on Mr. Cross. "I'm flattered that you want me for the lead role, but you haven't seen me dance."

"Oh, but I have. Before I created this dance troupe, I was on the Oregon Ballet Theater's hiring committee. You are more than qualified. When you declined the job at OBT, I had little hope you'd be interested in mine, but your friend Gavin said you might be persuaded."

My dad would've been so proud. I sucked in a large breath, my heart thudding loud in my ears. "Mr. Cross, I'd love to join your troupe."

"Splendid! Someone will contact you with the details. I look forward to your performances, and tell Gavin thanks for the tip." Before I could respond, he ended the call.

I stared at my phone for several long seconds, the display blurring in my vision.

Gavin brushed his fingers down my arm, dragging my attention to him. "Alexandra—"

I didn't give him time to finish. Instead, I threw my arms around his waist, holding him tight. My tears dampened his shirt.

He rubbed his fingers over my back, relaxing me in that special Gavin way.

"Thank you," I whispered.

He drew me away and cupped my face in both his palms. "There isn't anything I wouldn't do for you."

My chest expanded, love for him rising up from my soul. "And I, for you."

A soft knock then the slight creak of the door filled the air. The scent of cherry lotion washed over me. My attention flicked to the new arrival. A young woman with long jet-black hair, a dark mini-skirt, and a faux lace bodice stepped into the room. *A blood courtesan.*

Her gaze travelled between me and Gavin then darted around the room. She rubbed her bare arms, worry lines forming around her eyes. "Is Max here?"

I had no idea Max enjoyed courtesans. A smile tugged at my lips. Later, I'd tease him good about this. I drew my fingers down Gavin's arm and gave him a squeeze before I approached the new courtesan. "No, Max isn't here. What's your name and how did you get in?"

"My name is Laura." She shuffled her feet and drew her lip between her teeth. "Max dropped me off, said he had to park the car in the back and for me to meet him in the kitchen. I got lost and—"

I touched her arm. "It's a big house, I certainly understand how you could lose your way. I'm sure Max will be along any moment. Would you like a drink? We have champagne, wine, beer, or any assortment of hard liquors. Oh, and water if you prefer."

The tension in her shoulders eased. "Thank you. Water would be fine."

Her attention turned to Gavin and a flicker of fear rippled over her features. I handed her a bottle and whispered, "Don't mind him. He's as gentle as a kitten."

"I heard that." Gavin's deep chuckle slid into my senses, teasing me.

Heavy footsteps pounded in the hall. A moment later, Max stood in the doorway. His gaze drew to Laura then flicked to me then Gavin. He stepped into the room and ran his hand through his hair. "I'm sorry, Gavin, Lexi. I didn't mean for—"

Gavin's laughter reverberated off the walls. "Max, my dear friend. Have you kept secrets from us?"

He coughed, his focused attention flicking to the new courtesan. "We stopped by for some of Ester's famous cookies…"

I smiled, enjoying Max's unease.

Gavin stepped toward Max and clapped him on the back. "Sure you did. If you wanted to use the kitchen or the hot tub or one of the spare bedrooms, all you had to do was ask."

Max's shoulders eased. "Thanks, man. Laura, let's go."

Laura set her drink on the bar and scurried to Max, her high heels clicking on the wood floor.

As they left, my laughter melded with Gavin's. He met me in the middle of the room and scooped me into his arms. As he twirled me around, a profound happiness filled me to the deepest part of my soul. I'd found the man of my dreams and a love ever-lasting.

Enjoyed reading Lexi and Gavin's story? Want to read more from Rosalie? Delve into the war over Earth's most precious resource —water—and the fate of humankind in the *Warriors of Lemuria* COMPLETE series. Read more for a sneak peek at book 1, ***Untouchable Lover***.

SNEAK PEEK - UNTOUCHABLE LOVER

BOOK 1 IN THE WARRIORS OF LEMURIA SERIES

SOMEWHERE IN THE PACIFIC NORTHWEST MOUNTAINS

PRESENT DAY

CHAPTER 1

Stale air and mildew assailed Melissa's nose. She tried to swallow, but the thick smell coated her throat. Lifting her head, she opened her eyes. Light blinded her, sending a sharp jolt of pain through her skull. *Where am I?*

She stood erect, her backside pressed against a solid, cold surface. Dampness coated her skin. A thin line of drool spilled from her mouth and onto her chin. She raised her hand to wipe the wetness away, only to discover chains bound her wrists. The iron manacles rattled, echoing off the cement walls. A drop of fear weaseled its way into her mind. She inhaled, and a wave of dizziness passed over her.

The pungent smell of rubbing alcohol filtered into the cell, the telltale sign of Gossum. Melissa's throat constricted, and she gagged. She'd never get used to that stench, not as long as she lived. She winced. That might not be for much longer.

Memories of the Gossum attack raised her pulse and made her shiver. She didn't want to think about why this had happened, why she'd left the safety of her Pride, but she couldn't stop herself. Her heart clenched, and she choked back a sob.

She'd left Denver in search of another Pride, one where maybe, just maybe, she'd be accepted for who she was and not ridiculed for being different. As the only Dren in recent memory to conceive and birth a child, the rest of the Pride either hated her from petty jealousy or wanted to own her. She'd traveled as far as Portland, Oregon, before her need to feed drove her to seek a human male.

Luring a man out of a grocery store late at night, she couldn't bring herself to drink from him. He would've found the sensation pleasurable, and she wouldn't have taken enough blood to kill him, but the human frailty reflected in his eyes, and his likeness to William, her dead mate, had squashed any desire of feeding. She'd fled the scene as far as her feet would take her.

Her enemy found her as she'd stumbled into the warehouse district. Weak from her unwillingness to feed, she wasn't able to maintain her shield. They'd caught her between the old brick buildings. She shuddered at the recollection.

Denver seemed so far away. A ball of regret grew in her stomach. If she'd stayed, she'd be Demir's concubine by now. As ruler of the Pride, he'd wanted her to come to him on her own. When she hadn't, he'd become so enraged she'd feared for her life. What would become of her now? Despair lodged itself in her chest, festering, building until a layer of sweat coated her body.

"Don't fear. They can smell it," a masculine voice said. "They'll be back soon enough."

Across the room, a tall male stood shackled to the wall. Not only did he have arm and leg chains, but cuffs surrounded his neck and torso as well. One arm had a design etched into his skin that ended with four dark lines down the back of his hand. Intelligence shone from one pale blue eye. The other one was darkened with bruising and swollen shut. He looked like he'd seen more than his share of pain and heartache. His short brown hair had a spot of grey, and the lines in his face indicated he wasn't young. Neither Gossum nor human, he was a species she'd never met.

"Who are you—and where are we?" she asked.

"I'm Gaetan. We're in the Gossum's care, so to speak." His voice was rough, strained.

"Why capture us? Why not just kill us?" The bastard Gossum killed her mate and young son the year before. Her mind fought the horrific images and memories, anything to stop her from going insane with grief. She bit the side of her mouth to stifle a wail of sorrow. Still, a soft whimper escaped.

"That is the question of the hour," he said.

Cuts and bruises marred his arms and legs. When he breathed, his breaths were shallow as if he were in great pain. His left leg was smaller than his right and misshapen, forcing him to lean to the left. They had tortured him. When would they come back to finish the job?

Footsteps approached from the hallway. She tensed, and her pulse pounded in tune with each step.

A Gossum's massive body filled the entrance to her cell. The light from the corridor illuminated him from behind, and his face was a mask of shadows. He snickered. The low sound chilled her arms.

The large male stepped into the chamber, and his features became visible in the dim light. His grim face accentuated his bulbous nose. The brim of his cap covered the back of his neck.

From prior experience with Gossum, she knew he wore the hat to hide his bald head and the beginning of the hard scales that ran down his back. Although once human, he no longer required his eyelids to protect his hard, lizard-like, black eyes. They reflected the light with an eerie shine.

"Ah, good, you're awake. Are you ready to chat?" His menacing voice rasped with venom.

Melissa clamped her lips tight. The steady drip of water nearby echoed against the bare walls. Her damp hair hung in her eyes, the bitterly cold strands clung to her cheeks and arms.

His face turned red at her silence, but he remained calm. He leaned against the wall and crossed his arms. His yellow and black high-tops stood out like a beacon. He could still pass as human, given the right clothing to cover his hairless body and neck scales.

"Ignoring me won't help your cause," he said.

"Don't give in to his demands." Gaetan pulled against his chains.

Their jailer sauntered over to Gaetan. "Still with us, I see." He touched Gaetan's face, raking a claw over his cheek.

Gaetan snarled, and his good eye glowed with specks of gold.

"Oh, yeah, we're making progress." The vile creature chuckled. He turned toward Melissa, and a chilling smile revealed his serrated teeth, the ones he hid from the humans.

She shivered at the sight. Her life couldn't end this way, at the hands of her enemy. Memories of Seth and William raced through her mind, and a knot of determination formed in her stomach. She would fight for them, to honor their memory.

She yanked on her chains but only succeeded in opening cuts on her wrists. Blood trickled over her arm and dripped onto the concrete floor. She wanted to scream her rage at the Gossum, but she held her anger in check, barely.

Like a black cloud, their captor's presence filled the room. Even in his nonchalance his gaze pierced her, held her in place, while a cool bead of sweat rolled down the back of her neck. She feared him, but she wouldn't give her tormentor the satisfaction of seeing her weakness.

"Tell me your name, my dear." His soft and encouraging voice belied his evil intent.

She refused to speak, and instead, raised her chin.

"C'mon now, how is telling me your name going to hurt?" The corner of his mouth pulled into a smile. He returned to Gaetan and pointed, a claw extending like a crooked tree branch from his bony finger near the prisoner's good eye. "I like the sound of his howl. Would you like to hear it?"

Heat flushed through her body. Hatred burned in her gut for what they'd done to Gaetan. She wouldn't be the cause of more pain.

"Melissa," she spat. "My name is Melissa."

"Ah, much better. My name is Ram. Now we are acquainted." Ram placed his index finger next to his mouth and looked at the ceiling. "So, Melissa, about that shield of yours. I could do so much with it."

Melissa flinched at the mention of her gift. She tried to power her energy, but there wasn't even a spark. She held Ram's gaze and struggled to control her shaking knees.

"It's too bad I need you alive to get your blood. Lemurians disintegrate so quickly once dead that I can't get it fast enough." Ram tsked. "So, I'll give you a chance to cooperate."

"I won't give my shield to you." Melissa curled her hands into fists. He wanted her magical power, but no way would she give her special skill to the enemy.

Ram's smile turned into a grimace, and his easygoing demeanor evaporated. He became rigid, his muscles bunching in his arms and legs. His elongated tongue whipped in and out of his mouth, the dangerous spur at the tip coming close to her face.

She recoiled, and her head struck the hard cement wall. Stars swam in her vision, but she refused to succumb to the darkness. Dread snaked its way into her heart.

"As you wish." Ram snapped his fingers.

One of his brood entered the room carrying a cast iron

bucket. The top of a branding iron extended over the lip. A towel wrapped around the end protected the handle from the heat within the kettle. The smell of smoldering coal joined with the odors of sweat and fear.

Melissa's pulse quickened. She swallowed, but nothing went down. Her throat was too parched.

Ram grabbed the branding iron.

Adrenaline rushed through her body. "Wh-what is that for?"

"It's your incentive."

"No, don't, not her. Take me." Gaetan's voice, weak and rough, carried across the room.

Melissa glanced at him. They'd just met, but his willingness to protect her spoke volumes about his character.

Ram snapped to attention. "Oh, I intend to get what I need from you, Stiyaha. That abnormal strength of yours will be mine, just not yet. I will take her gift first."

Ram turned his focus back to Melissa. "I want your shield, and I want it now."

He closed the distance, the branding iron's heat radiating in the space between them. Her legs shook, making the shackles at her ankles clank together like an eerie wind chime. Her fear ratcheted up another level, sending a shiver of terror over her shoulders. She hated him all the more.

"Are you willing to bargain? Or are you going to be stubborn?" Ram leaned in, and his breath reeked of liquor. "I know you're Lemurian, but you're not Stiyaha. You must not be from around here. Tell me what you are," he purred, as he drew the back of a finger down the side of her face.

She flinched at his touch, but she wouldn't let him intimidate her. Making eye contact with her enemy, she held her ground.

"If you lead me to others like you, I'll let you walk away, unscathed," he said.

She bared her fangs. "I would never sell out my kind. I will fight you every step of the way."

"Well, now, that's what I thought you'd say." His eyes gleamed with delight, and his mouth curved into a grin. "Let's play, shall we?"

For more information on *Untouchable Lover*, visit www.rosalieredd.com.

Books in the *Warriors of Lemuria* COMPLETE series:
Unforgettable Lover - stand-alone novella
Untouchable Lover - book #1
Untamable Lover - book #2
Unimaginable Lover - book #3
Undeniable Lover - book #4
Unforgivable Lover - book #5
Alora's Love Potion - short story collection
Marked by Love - stand-alone novella

Other books by Rosalie Redd:
Clone Me a Lover - Interstellar Lovers book #1

ABOUT ROSALIE

After finishing a rewarding career in finance and accounting, it was time for award-winning author Rosalie Redd to put away the spreadsheets and take out the word processor. She pens paranormal, science fiction, and fantasy romance in her office cave located in Oregon, where rain is just another excuse to keep writing.